Aliens of the third realm

Deborah Emery

Dedication

To my husband Waynne who supports me in all my writing endeavors and allowed me to pick his brain for the scientific and technical information. Special thanks goes to Wally and Elizabeth for guiding me on the more current alien information. To Bronwyn, Jody, Zac, and, Megan, for allowing me to be creative with them in my story.

Aliens of the third realm

Bronwyn was finally taking her vacation. Her mother had not wanted her to travel the United States without a companion. "A young woman of 23 years should not drive around this country alone", Bronwyn's mother had said, but Bronwyn promised to check in often. "Often", stated Bronwyn's mother, "how often is often?" Bronwyn promised to call in the morning at 10:00 a.m. and in the evening around 4:00 p.m. Although Bronwyn's mother still wasn't happy about her only daughter driving around the United States by herself, Bronwyn was an adult and had every right to make her own decisions.

Bronwyn, nicked named Wynnie, had wanted to visit every state in the U.S. She had driven up through New York and saw Niagara Falls. The magnificent flow of force from the water was amazing. She made it to Maine to see the famous Bar Harbor and the beautiful waves of the Atlantic Ocean. How tranquil the rhythmic ocean waves could be. She then traveled downward and west visiting all the states around Lake Erie. She had visited the Dakotas and viewed the majestic Mount Rushmore. She went through Washington State and down through Oregon to California to see the giant red wood trees. The enormous trees were beyond description.

Wynnie now drove down the scenic coast of California. The Pacific Ocean view was breath taking. "I wish I had all the time in the world to see all the wonderful things each state can offer", Wynnie said to herself. Vacation time was getting short, so she studied her map. I can see the caverns in New Mexico on my way back home. Finishing her salad, she paid her bill and headed for her car. She then took another glance at the map and drove toward the expressway.

It wasn't long before Wynnie was parked in the parking lot of one of New Mexico's well-advertised caverns. She called her mother. The call went to voice mail. "Hi Mom, I'm just checking in. I am going to visit a cavern today. I plan on staying the night in New Mexico and then drive as far as I can tomorrow. I should see you in about three days. I miss you and dad but I'll see you soon".

Wynnie locked the car and walked to the entrance of the cavern. Several other people were standing in line. A group was gathering for a guided tour down through the caverns. Wynnie decided to go with the tour. She paid for her ticket, used the facilities, and then stood at the end of the line. It wasn't long before the tour guide stood in front of the group. "Welcome. We always enjoy showing off our natural treasures to new people. Can you tell me where you are from?" asked the guide.

Beginning at the front of the line, people rattled off the city and state they were from. Wynnie spoke up when her turn came. The guide then asked if everyone had a partner in which to walk the trails of the cavern paths. Wynnie admitted she was alone. The guide stated, that he would have her walk next to him to ensure her safety. "Every once in a while, we have a person wander off the trail path in order to get a closer view of one of our formations. That is why we ask people to walk in pairs. The second person can call for help if one person somehow manages to become lost", stated the guide.

The guide then handed everyone in the group a brochure which included a map of the cavern trails and the various formations of the cavern. The guide carried a flashlight to signal the way. Although rails were added to areas that appeared to drop downward, small dim lights could be seen fixed to the walls of the cavern to offer the visitor a little help in remaining safely on the trails. The guide walked with Wynnie beside him. The trail slowly descended downward. The guide warned everyone that the trail would be making a descent and that the more exciting formations were deeper in the ground. Health warnings for those who may have issues walking up hill on the return trip was also announced. Everyone voiced they were fine to make the walk.

The group had been walking for about a half hour when all the small lights suddenly went out. A woman in the group shrieked. The guide spoke, "please stay where you are everyone. Every once in a while, the cavern loses a stalactites and it seems to aim for the wires of the lights. Our back up lighting will kick in shortly. Just have a little patience", stated the guide. Someone took Wynnie's hand. She assumed it was the guide. She began walking blindly led by the hand that now held hers. Fearful of where they were walking, Wynnie took very small steps. They continued to walk slowly but seemed to follow the trail downward. Suddenly a rag was placed over her nose. She breathed in an awful scent which made her head go fuzzy. She fought the sleepiness that had suddenly come on, but she couldn't stay awake. Her eyes closed.

When Wynnie awoke, she was lying on large table. The table was similar to those she had seen on television in hospital scenes. Her arms were secured to her side and her legs were elevated and separated. Her feet were secure in little metal stirrups. She had no idea what was going on. She began to scream. A man seemed to suddenly appear. He placed something over Wynnie's nose and she fell back to sleep.

Paul sat in his car listening to his portable police scanner. Paul was a newspaper reporter and one of the city's best. He always managed to out scoop and out write most of the reporters on other competitive papers. Paul was able to find his great stories to write about thanks to his portable police scanner. Paul was usually first on the scene of any significant event announced over the police radio. He interviewed victims and responders alike, making his newspaper stories more detailed and personal. The radio squawked, "A woman states her daughter visited a cavern in New Mexico and never checked back in. Please send a car to investigate", stated the police dispatcher.
"The caverns aren't that far away, I'll swing by there and see what pans out before heading back to the paper", stated Paul to himself.

Paul arrived at the cavern entrance. He followed the signs to the parking lot. After he had driven around the lot a few times, he noticed a car that matched the description that the police dispatcher had stated was that of the missing girl. Paul pulled out his digital camera and took a few photos. The photos always made his story more authentic. Paul parked nearby and grabbed his note pad and began jotting down a few notes. Paul noticed a man walking through the parking lot in his direction. The man opened the car door of the missing girl's car, started the motor, and drove the care away. Paul took another look at the camera's picture menu and retrieved the recent pictures. He checked the license plate number. The license plate number was a match for the missing girl's car.

Perplexed, Paul drove to the nearest police station. "Was the girl in the car?" asked the officer.

"I have no idea. I didn't see anyone except the man", stated Paul, "I arrived and saw the car parked in the lot. I took a few pictures and was just going to jot down a few notes when this guy comes out of nowhere and drives off in the car. I have no idea where he drove the car or if he was alone when he drove off". Paul showed the police officer the digital pictures of the car and points out the license plate number.

"See, it's a match", stated Paul. The officer looked at Paul and stated, "We'll check it out".

Paul was frustrated at best. "I show them it's the girl's car, where it was parked, and all I get is we'll check it out. I think I may need to check this situation out myself", he said to himself. He went back to his job site and picked up the telephone. "Archives, can you get me all the information you can on the caverns in New Mexico?" A file soon was dropped on Paul's desk. He browsed through the file. "Hmm, reports of aliens in the area. Not illegal aliens but aliens from space. Yeah, right", Paul mumbled to himself. Then he noticed another report about a contractor for the government had been building a storage bunker underground. It seems a battle ensued between the contractor and aliens. All this happened around the caverns too. "I think I need to investigate this situation further. There just may be an alien story in my future".

"Paul", stated Jody, "Amy said you called. What's up?"
"Oh, hey Jody, I wanted to pick your brain", stated Paul.
"Not much left these days", laughed Jody.
"I know one of your hobbies is gathering information on U.F.O., aliens, and stuff like that. Can you tell me anything about the suspected aliens in the area of the caverns? "Asked Paul.
"Hobby? If you talk to Amy, it's an obsession", replied Jody.
"Can you give me some information on the local findings?" asked Paul.

"Sure", stated Jody "I have tons of stuff stored in my desk. Come on". Paul followed Jody down the hall to Jody's office. Jody opened up his bottom drawer to reveal dozens and dozens of files. Jody pulled out several folders. "This file has interviews from an ex-military man who swears he was under orders to keep silent about the aliens he was guarding. And before you ask, he says he believes the public has the right to know what is going on".

As Paul began reading some of the notes, he asked, "Can we get in touch with him?"

"He contacts local papers when he wants to talk. I have no way of knowing where he is. I don't even know his name. He uses alias names and interviews in various locations. He has reported to seeing aliens developing in pod-like containers. He said these aliens have been helping our government in some way", stated Jody.

"Helping how?" asked Paul.

"Technology for one", replied Jody as he picked up another file. "This file has paper clippings of UFO spotting and even mentions Roswell connections, and the caverns. Oh yeah, there was even mention of a battle that happened with a government contractor who ran into some kind of evil lizard-like alien. I think the contractor was building an underground storage facility".

"I think I recently started reading about that. Where was that?" Asked Paul as he continued to scan over the contents of various folders.

"I forget", replied Jody, "I do remember the lizard guy had some kind of laser gun. The contractor ended up destroying the facility to prevent the alien from escaping into our world or above ground", stated Jody.

"How far back does your information go? "Ask Paul.

"I collected the more recent stories. My collection goes back to when I first started here. So maybe 15 to 20 years or so. Remember Zac? That really smart kid who worked here for about a year and a half or so?" asked Jody."

"I think so. Wasn't he actually going to college to become a musician? Yeah, I remember him, why", Asked Paul.

"Because Zac got engaged to Megan. Megan's dad was one of those early internet gurus. He was really internet savvy. He collected a lot of alien and UFO material. Zac gave me a ton of stuff that Megan's dad was getting rid of. I guess Megan's dad put all his information on flash drives or DVDs. He even had some of that blue book stuff", exclaimed Jody.

"I guess I'm asking the wrong questions. When did aliens first appear on earth or at least the first documentation of aliens?" Asked Paul.

"In biblical times. Many of the early writings speak of aliens coming to earth. Our women were so beautiful and so these beings came down to mate with them. Then there is the theory that some early humans were genetically altered to make slaves", stated Jody.

"Genetically altered? That sounds a bit farfetched", replied Paul.

"Well apparently our blood cells have an Rh factor. Most of the planet is Rh positive", said Jody.

"Rh positive. What does Rh stand for and how does it tie in with the alien theory? "Asked Paul.

"Rh stands for rhesus factor. It's a protein on the red blood cell. If you don't have the protein on your red blood cells, you are Rh negative. Funny thing is they discovered Rh negative is resistant to HIV. Theory has it, Rh negative people are the descendants of genetically altered people. These people were altered by aliens to ensure they would be able to resist infections, be able to work hard, and live a long time", stated Jody.

"So what happened to these aliens? "Asked Paul.

"Couldn't survive in our atmosphere. We have too many germs. Remember that movie? Oh, what was the name of that thing? Oh, yeah, war of the worlds. I think the movie was based on that belief", replied Jody.

"Ok, so why do they stay here then?" Asked Paul.

"There are several theories on that one" answered Jody.

"Like what?" Asked Paul.

"They are genetically altering their own race to resist our germs", stated Jody.

"Why and how?" Asked Paul.

"To answer both, I'm not sure. Some of my group believe they are kidnapping humans and using their blood to develop vaccines against our germs", said Jody.

"Group? You have a group and how could the alien's possibly do any of that? Where would the aliens do that?" Asked Paul.

"Yes, there are many groups that believe in aliens. Anyone can become a member. As for where the aliens are now, they could be located just about anywhere", replied Jody,

"How can they take humans without it being detected?" Asked Paul.

"I'll answer that question with a question. Did you know that serial killers are less likely to get caught if they strike in the rural or country areas then if they struck in a very populated area?" asked Jody.

"What does that have to do with my question?" Asked Paul.

"I guess the same would hold true of missing persons. Anyone who goes missing may not be detected or reported", replied Jody.

"That makes sense, actually. People in rural areas want to move to big cities. If they disappeared, it may seem as though they ran off", suggested Paul.

"Funny how all this starts to come together. Almost like a puzzle", replied Jody.

"Any idea where the aliens actually live?" Asked Paul.

"That is anyone's guess. It would have to be somewhere in which they could get food, water, and air. And of course, not be discovered or be exposed to human germs", replied Jody.

"We don't know what technology they actually have. They could possibly live under the ocean or mountainous regions", suggested Paul.

"Not likely. They'd be seen by our satellites. If they developed a vaccine that would work, they may be living among us now and we wouldn't even know it", stated Jody.

"Do you think they wish us harm?" Asked Paul.

"Hard to say. The lizard with the laser may have been protecting himself and his home. Maybe they are afraid of us", suggested Jody.

"Ok, so why stay here?" Asked Paul.

"Why not? Earth is a great planet. We see other planets, stars, and other spacial bodies in pictures from space cameras. Ever see one with water or a livable environment? My guess would be that Earth has everything they need. Well, except us", replied Jody.

"Now that you mention it. What about us humans?" asked Paul.

"That is the million dollar question, isn't it? Some believe we would be slaves or food for the aliens. Maybe both", stated Jody.

When Wynnie awoke, she was in an unfamiliar room. The room was stone like. There were no doors or windows. The room had the bed she was now lying in, a single table and chair, and a florescent ceiling. There was a plate filled with food and a cup filled with a beverage on the table. Suddenly the distant wall began to move inward. A man entered and the wall closed behind him. "I am Rudy. I am the leader of my group. I know you must have a lot of questions".

"We are poor people. We don't have much money. We live pay check to pay check. There is no way my parents can afford to pay a ransom", stated Wynnie.

"Let me explain why we have brought you here. You will be given every opportunity to have your questions answered" replied Rudy. "Long ago, my race came to your planet. We had been banished from our world because we found the people of earth so beautiful. We marveled at your skin colors. People with skin the colors of pink, brown, yellow, and red. Your bodies were warm and soft too. Although your earth was a young planet, my group decided to stay here. We were a small group and my people were becoming extinct. Our elders held a meeting and decided we needed to enlarge our group. You have been brought here or recruited to be a donor".

Wynnie's eyes widened. "What does that mean?"
"We harvest your eggs and remove your DNA. We inject our DNA into the egg and then fertilize the egg with our sperm. We have surrogate women who are perfect breeders", exclaimed Rudy.

"Earth women? "Asked Wynnie.

"Of course", stated Rudy, "I have already said there are not enough of my population to survive. Earth women have been chosen to help us".

"That's against the law", responded Wynnie.

"They have volunteered", replied Rudy, "There are some of your citizens that actually seek us out".

"I don't believe you", replied Wynnie.

"I give you no reason to mistrust me", stated Rudy.
"You kidnapped me, you sucked out my eggs without my permission, and you are holding me here against my will. That gives me reason enough to mistrust you", stated Wynnie.
"My race must survive. Yes, we did bring you here. We did harvest a few of your eggs. However; you may walk around freely but I'm afraid you may never leave. We cannot have our existence known or it will create problems", exclaimed Rudy.
"Can't you erase my memory and let me go?" asked Wynnie.
"We do not have that type of technology", replied Rudy.
"My parents will be sick with worry. You have no right", screamed Wynnie.
"What is done, is done. You must make the best of your situation. You will be treated well. We need you healthy so your donations will be of good quality", explained Rudy.
"You are stealing my life", replied Wynnie.
"We are finished with this conversation. May I show you around? You may want to meet some of the citizens we have here", replied Rudy.
Even though Wynnie didn't want to be there, she thought if she learned her way around, she may be able to find a way to escape. Wynnie followed Rudy through the opening that was a wall of what would now be her room. "Remember your way", she said to herself.
"How far down are we?" Wynnie asked.
Ignoring her questions, Rudy began to explain the area. "Over there, you can see fields of vegetation. The vegetation is not like your vegetation above ground but you will acquire a taste for it", stated Rudy. Wynnie looked at rows of vegetation. It looked like large bean sprouts and white tomatoes. "Of course, this is only one of many areas of food growth", informed Rudy. They continued to walk and Wynnie saw a large lake.

"The lake is our drinking water. Your earth collects water on the surface and it is filtered through the ground. We collect it here for our use", replied Rudy.

Wynnie looked around. No paths that led upward could be seen. Rudy continued walking. They entered another area. The sound of babies crying echoed throughout the cavern. The sound grew louder as they walked. Rudy led Wynnie into a room filled with crying babies. There were several babies in small square beds. The babies' skin were golden in color and all the babies had hair that was pale white. The Babies were naked without diapers or blankets.

"The babies' sound hungry", replied Wynnie.

"Yes, they will be fed soon", responded Rudy.

Suddenly a short, gray creature, wearing no clothes entered the room. The creature had long arms and legs and walked quickly. The gray creature placed strips of meat into the babies' mouths.

"Our babies are much more advanced than Earth babies. Our babies need high protein in the first years of life, then vegetation is added to their diet. Earth babies are so disabled. They drink liquids for months before being introduced to vegetation, then need more time before being introduced to protein. That is yet another reason our race must survive, we are superior", exclaimed Rudy.

Wynnie remained silent. They continued to walk. Then Wynnie heard screaming.

"Do not concern yourself with the noise. The surrogate mothers are delivering our babies".

They entered into an area with approximately eight naked women. The women were sitting in chair-like devices. There was a small board for the women to rest the back of their buttock on but the rest of the seat of the chair was open. Beneath each chair was a huge sponge-like square.

"All of these women volunteered to give birth to your babies?" questioned Wynnie.

"Given the alternative, yes. They volunteered", replied Rudy.

"What is the alternative?" asked Wynnie.

"Death", said Rudy as if it was of little importance.

"What happens to these women when they can no longer bear children?" asked Wynnie.

"We find other uses for them", stated Rudy.

"How did they come here in the first place?" asked Wynnie.

"The same way you did. It is a process", replied Rudy.

"A process?" questioned Wynnie," How long has this process been going on? "Asked Wynnie.

Rudy ignored her question. "We retrieve young women. First we harvest donor eggs from our volunteers. When the egg supply is exhausted, the woman becomes a surrogate. Once the woman can no longer bear children, we find other uses for them", claimed Rudy.

"What other uses?" asked Wynnie, "and how long does it take for the egg supply to become exhausted?"

"Farming, cleaning, pleasure services, cooking, caring for our elders, and waste management", replied Rudy. Suddenly, one of the women screamed. A large gelatinous egg shaped item dropped to the sponge below. The gelatinous material began to melt away. Wynnie watched with morbid curiosity. The remaining form was a very large head with slanted eyes and a small body. The woman who had given birth cried. "Let me die. I don't want to grow anymore of your creatures", she screamed.

A tall, yet amazingly beautiful blonde woman entered. The blonde woman wore no clothes. Her body was well developed and it did not seem to bother her that everyone watched her as she moved toward the screaming woman. The blonde woman placed something in the screaming woman's mouth. The screaming woman spit it out. "No, not anymore", screamed the woman.

The blonde woman grabbed the screaming woman by the neck. The blonde women's long pale fingers wrapped almost entirely around the screaming woman's throat. The screaming woman was now silent. The woman tried to scream but nothing came out. The blonde woman shoved something into the woman's mouth and said, "Swallow".

The woman tried to spit out whatever had been placed in her mouth. The blonde woman shoved two very long fingers into the woman's mouth. The woman choked and eventually swallowed the capsule. It seemed only a few moments had passed when the woman began to relax and finally stilled. A short gray colored creature rushed in and collected the newborn alien.

Rudy ushered Wynnie out of the birthing room. "That woman didn't volunteer. What did you drug her with?" asked Wynnie.

"A combination of a fertility stimulant and an endorphin enhancer. She will be ready to serve again in a few weeks", stated Rudy casually.

"Her body can't recover that quickly. Even a year could be too soon", stated Wynnie.

"You do not understand. The women are here for our use. If her body wears out, we will find a different use for her", rationalized Rudy calmly.

 I need to find a way out of here, thought Wynnie to herself. Wynnie clenched her fist to prevent Rudy from seeing how much her hands were trembling.

"Where does your race live?" asked Wynnie.

"We are several levels above. You and the other women have your own rooms on this level. You may walk around but you must not venture off this level", instructed Rudy.

"Why can't we visit your level?" asked Wynnie.

"As I have stated before, humans have too many pathogens that can cause us harm", stated Rudy.

Wynnie could feel fear growing inside. Rudy lead Wynnie back to her assigned room. He showed her how to open her door. It was actually a small wall that would pivot open similar to that of a revolving door. Rudy also explained when her meals would be served and showed her a small door that opened to a bathroom like room, which included a bath tub and a portable toilet.

"Water is brought in daily. The large container near the toilet has a large ladle. When you finish urinating or defecating, ladle water into the toilet bowel to clear the waste. Ladle water over you in the tub to bath", instructed Rudy.

"What about clothes? I'll need clean clothes to wear", stated Wynnie.

"Wear the clothes you have on or go without. It is of no consequence here. The temperature down here is always sixty eight degrees. No one cares of your appearance. Even my race does not require garments, as you have seen", stated Rudy. Rudy stood about six foot one. His body was lean but muscular. He wore loose material around his waist that draped and covered his genitals. He wore no shirt and his skin was pale. His hair was shoulder length and white. His eyes were dark and slightly slanted. "I will leave you to explore your new environment", stated Rudy as he turned to leave. When the door to her room closed, Wynnie sat on the bed and whispered, "So, I have one month before they will force me to donate my eggs again. I need to find a way out of here, and as soon as possible". Wynnie decided she needed to calmly plan her escape. "I'll need a light. I may need food and water too. I have no idea how long it will take me to get back up to the surface", she said to herself.

Wynnie had no idea if it were day or night. Someone had apparently removed her watch. Wynnie pushed open the door and turned to the right. Rudy had led her on a path leading left out of her room. The walk way had narrowed then abruptly ended. Wynnie pushed on the rock but there was no movement. The area was not very well lit. "Maybe one of the other women may have some knowledge of how to get out of here", Wynnie said to herself.

Wynnie walked back down the path. She passed her assigned room and headed toward the delivery room. There were five women still in active labor.

"Are you all ok"? Asked Wynnie. They looked exhausted.

"Can I get you some water"? Asked Wynnie.

"We aren't allowed anything to eat or drink until we deliver", stated a thirty year old woman.

"My name is Wynnie. This is my first day in this place", Wynnie explained nervously.

"I'm Donna. Jessie is the gal with the red hair", said Donna as she slanted her head to the right. A contraction that seemed to last forever stopped Donna from talking.

"How long have you been here"? Asked Wynnie.

"We've lost track of time", stated Cindy, the woman next to Donna.

Suddenly Donna screamed and arched her body. The egg shaped item dropped onto the sponge below. The gelatin-like substance began to melt away. The beautiful blonde woman appeared. She placed a capsule in Donna's mouth. Donna was crying as she swallowed. A short gray creature raced in and collected the alien baby. The blonde woman looked at Wynnie then turned and walked away.

Wynnie was expecting Donna to deliver an after-birth, but instead Donna stood and slowly walked to the corner of the room. Donna ladled a drink of water. Wynnie could see traces of blood on Donna's legs.

"Can I help you to your room"? Asked Wynnie.

"We aren't allowed help. If we can't get to our rooms, they will no longer need us. If they no longer can use us, they get rid of us", exclaimed Donna.

"Rudy said you are given a different job if you can no longer do child birthing", stated Wynnie.

"Yeah, a different job", laughed Donna sarcastically.

Wynnie thought she'd throw up. Donna slowly moved into the pathway and headed toward the rooms. Wynnie wandered around. There wasn't much too really see. She did notice some of the pathways had shorter walls than the others. Rudy had to leave somehow. Wynnie climbed on one of the short walls. There seemed to be small spots in the rock that were similar to that on rock climbing walls. Wynnie would wait and check it out when she felt the area would be less likely to have people or creatures walking by. There were still several women in active labor.

"The labor area, of course", thought Wynnie. The blonde woman and gray creatures were entering the birthing room from the back. Maybe there was a back entrance. Wynnie went back to her room. Why are the baby aliens kept on this level? Rudy didn't want us humans giving them human germs. It doesn't make sense. Where do they get the meat for those alien babies? Do the aliens grown livestock too?

The door of Wynnie's room opened. A human woman pushed in a cart with vegetation on it. "Is there anything to drink"? Asked Wynnie.

"Didn't Rudy show you the water basin with the ladle"? Asked the woman.

"He said it was to flush the toilet or take a bath", replied Wynnie.

"That too. You drink it, you use it to wash with and to flush", stated the woman.

"My name is Wynnie", said Wynnie to the woman.

"Stella", replied the woman as she turned to leave.

"How long have you been here"? Asked Wynnie

"Years. How many, I can't tell you. It's easy to lose track of time in here", replied Stella.

"How long have you been serving meals"? Asked Wynnie.

"After they removed all my eggs, they tried me as a surrogate but my body kept miscarrying. They didn't want to waste their eggs so they made me a servant and occasionally a tool for pleasure", stated Stella.

"I'm afraid to ask what a tool for pleasure may entail", said Wynnie.

Stella lifted her shirt. Wynnie gasped in horror as she saw multiple bite marks on Stella's body.

"They give me something to numb the pain. They like the taste of human blood", stated Stella.

"Are they cannibals"? Asked Wynnie.

"I don't know. I don't know where they get the meat they feed their young. We get fed vegetables and water. They put supplements in the food for us too", replied Stella.

"How can you stand it"? Asked Wynnie.

"What choice is there"? Questioned Stella.

"Why not try and escape"? Asked Wynnie.

"One gal tried to escape once. I can't repeat what they did to her". Stated Stella.

"How did you find out they caught her and did something to her"? Asked Wynnie.

"They made us all watch", stated Stella. Stella then turned and left.

Paul decided he would have to investigate the cavern. "The girl's car was originally there. Maybe there is something going on at the caverns. I was thinking the girl may have gotten lost, but when that guy moved her car, it had to be a planned abduction. Maybe a white slavery ring. Human trafficking. Maybe she had an accident and they are trying to cover it up" he said to himself. He began to plot out a working plan. First, he would need supplies. He went to his apartment. He collected night goggles, glow sticks, some beef jerky, canned chicken, and six bottles of water. He placed all the equipment in a back pack. He added a hammer, some climbing ropes, levers, climbing gear, anchors, and a knife. "Now to wait until dusk", Paul said to himself. Paul ate a good dinner and then drove to the cavern parking lot. He chose to park in a parking spot a long way and to the side of the entrance. No one would notice if the car was left there or not. There were road trucks and hedge clippers parked in the lot. He pulled up behind the larges road truck which hid his car. "The county must use the parking lot too", he thought.

Wynnie tasted the vegetables that were on the cart that Stella had brought in. They were awful. She grabbed a handful of vegetables and rinsed them with water she had filled in the ladle. They tasted much better after being washed. After eating only a few vegetables, she felt tired. She laid down. She wasn't really sleepy but her head felt tipsy. "Maybe they put something in my food", Wynnie said to herself alarmed. Wynnie laid down and closed her eyes.

She heard her door open and Rudy's voice speaking to someone. "It seems the sedative has taken effect. Insert the yellow capsule each week on the same day after she eats her third meal. We will make certain her third meal of the day has been laced with sedatives so she will not awaken when you perform your job. We need her to sleep to give the capsule more time to work".

Wynnie had to keep pretending to sleep. "Breath slowly", Wynnie mentally told herself, "Remain calm".

Wynnie felt her pants being removed. Her panties were slide down and taken off as well. Wynnie prayed her blushing face would not show. "Breath slow. Stay calm", she kept telling herself. She felt something cool being pushed inside her. She had to fight the urge to scream. She had to endure this humiliation if she were going to get out of this place. She had to get away from these creatures. She just had too. Her pants and undergarments were left off. She listened. Her ears strained to make certain Rudy and his companion had left. She slowly opened her eyes. She was again alone. Wynnie raced to the bathroom. Inserting her fingers inside her vagina, she dug out the foreign capsule. She poured water from the ladle into her hand and splashed the water up inside. "I have to make certain to wash out whatever that thing was", she told herself. She shivered and began to gag. She began to wretch and vomited up what little she ate. "How could those other women put up this type of treatment"? She asked herself. "Tomorrow, I will explore the door on the other side of the delivery room. I have to find a way out. Oh, mom, I hope you are trying to find me", she said with a sob in her voice.

Wynnie was not usually emotional, but the strain of the situation and fear of her future had caught up to her and she wept. She cried hard and for a long time until she finally cried herself to sleep. Wynnie awoke to Stella tapping her on the arm.

"Breakfast time", Stated Stella. Breakfast was a bowl of green grainy mush.

"It looks awful, but it doesn't taste bad", Replied Stella. Wynnie's stomach growled. She was hungry but fear was greater.

"Do you eat this too"? Asked Wynnie as she stared into Stella's eyes.

"Yes, every morning", replied Stella.

Wynnie tasted it. It tasted like oatmeal. "I guess you just have to get past the way it looks", said Wynnie.

"You'll be surprised how much energy you'll have after you eat", stated Stella.

Stella left Wynnie to her breakfast. Wynnie waited a few minutes to ensure she didn't feel drugged, before eating the remainder of her breakfast.

Stella had been right. Wynnie did feel her energy level surged. She washed and dressed. "Now to check out the delivery room", she said to herself.

There were only three women in the delivery room. They looked exhausted. All the women were naked. How long those women had endured this breeding ritual was unthinkable.

"How long is your pregnancy"? Asked Wynnie.

"Once impregnated, the pregnancy last three months", replied a woman with very dark hair.

"Only three months"? Questioned Wynnie.

"They implant their seed and then pour in some type of fertilizer or food like gel. It feels like plaster. You feel like your body has been stretched. They force you to lay for two days after that procedure. After one week, you look like you are three months pregnant. When you sleep, you can hear strange sounds coming from within", explained the woman with dark hair.

Wynnie listened and felt herself becoming nauseated.

The woman continued, "After three months, you're stretched. You feel like you're going to explode. That is when the sharp shooting pains begin. You want to push but you can't. It's too big. It's not ready. That creature inside actually eats the afterbirth before shoving its way out. We pray each and every time they impregnate us that the creature within stops chewing after the afterbirth breaks free".

Wynnie paled.

"Afterward, we must walk to our rooms. They send a couple of those gray creatures to siphon our milk", said the dark haired woman, "They literally milk us for one week. Then make us eat this blue capsule that stops the milk production. The next day, they implant a capsule to help us heal and become ready for the next birth".

Wynnie felt the room spin. She grabbed one of the chairs and sat.

"You may as well know what you have to look forward to", replied the woman.

"I don't think I can do this", replied Wynnie.

"After having your body needled half to death for egg recovery, you may feel differently", said the woman.

"Surely, they must have enough of their population after all these years that they no longer need humans to be surrogates", stated Wynnie.

"Their woman decided they prefer not to give birth. They chose to have us supply them with their offspring", stated the woman.

"Why"? Questioned Wynnie.

"Sex to them is not pleasant. The male, when aroused, shoves his staff into the female. It has razor-like barbs on the end, or so I've been told. It anchors to the female's reproductive wall. It does not release for about twelve hours. During that time, the male will bite and suck blood to keep aroused. The males back bone can be maneuvered like that of a snake during their sexual experience. So the male can anchor himself and cause bleeding in the woman. He can twist his body so he can lap up that blood", explained the dark haired woman.

Wynnie closed her eyes. The thought was so revolting.

"If women have given up with mating, then what do the men do if they want to be sexually aroused"? Asked Wynnie.

"They will use human woman. Stella is one of the women they use. If they decide to use you, pray you don't bleed to death. Our body is designed to promote blood flow to our reproductive area. One cut can cause massive bleeding", replied the dark haired woman.

Wynnie had to force her breakfast back down.

"How can they hold us here"? Asked Wynnie.

"One gal tried to leave. They made us all stand and watch as they removed her skin, muscles, and drained her of her blood", stated the woman.

"That must have been awful for you", stated Wynnie.

"It was worse for the gal. She was alive when they started", replied the woman.

Wynnie could feel her legs shake. She was frightened beyond all belief. She managed to somehow make it back down the path toward her room before she collapsed in the walkway.

Paul managed to sneak past the one security guard that was guarding the entrance. He had to use the night vision goggles to see his way down the path into the cavern. He had to move slowly to ensure his footsteps would not be heard. He managed to pick up his pace once he left the immediate entrance area. He walked the path that steadily declined for almost an hour before stopping to catch his breath. It was then he heard voices. Paul managed to squeeze between two large stalagmites when a huge square of rock to his right began to move.

"You'll have to push the left side of this wall to open it", stated an older man to a younger man.

"When will we abduct our next human female"? Asked the younger man excitedly.

"When the time is right. The tour guide will ask each tour group where they are from. We prefer women from other parts of the country. The tour guide will then ask if everyone has a buddy to walk the cavern paths with. If a woman is alone, and lives far away from here, then she will be the target", explained the older man. The two men stood in front of the stone door.

"This is how you will exit our city and make your way to the chosen target. The tour guide will make certain the targeted woman is nearby", stated the older man.

"City"? Questioned Paul to himself.

"How did we get the tour guide to help us"? Asked the younger man.

"The tour guide and the guard have been persuaded, shall we say, to help us", stated the older man. The younger man nodded in acknowledgement. The two men then turned and exited the same way they had come. The door wall closing behind them.

Paul waited for several minutes before moving out of his hiding spot. Paul went to the stone wall that he now stood in front of and pushed the left side. The stone wall slowly moved. When there was an opening large enough to pass through, Paul stopped pushing and made his way through. Once on the other side, Paul pushed the wall door closed. Using the tip of his shoe, Paul scratched a mark that looked like an arrow in the dirt. "That should remind me where that passageway is", Paul said to himself. Paul could feel the strain of walking down hill on his knees but he kept moving. "This is going to make a great story".

Paul continued slowly walking on the path. He could see an occasional path leading to the right of the path he was currently on. "I'll stay on this path. It would be too easy to get lost if I veered off to the right", he told himself. He kept checking behind him to make certain no one could see him. The path dead ended at a wall. Paul pushed the left side of the wall and it slowly began to move. He again slipped through the doorway. "How deep does this path go"? Paul questioned. He continued to yet another dead end. He pushed on the wall and it too opened. Paul was stunned. He rubbed his eyes. There was a city beneath the ground. The roof of the cavern he had just entered glowed almost as if painted with one of those luminous paints. He could see dwelling after dwelling. Curious Paul continued to walk. "I wonder how many cities are down here". He asked himself.

Paul came to yet another wall that opened. This level had what looked like fields of tomatoes. Paul remained on the path. He came to yet another wall. It too opened. As he walked he could hear voices in the distance behind him. Paul pushed on a wall and it opened. Paul was stunned. On the ground ahead, lay a young beautiful woman. Paul kneeled. The woman was young, maybe twenty two or twenty three. He lifted the woman up and carried her toward the door he had just entered through. He attempted to prop the young woman up. "Wake up", he said as he gently patted Wynnie's face.

Wynnie's eyes slowly opened. "Who are you"? Asked Wynnie trying to get her bearings.

"I'm news reporter. I'm looking for a story, but I happened to find you. What are you doing here"? Asked Paul.

"I was kidnapped, as you very well know", replied Wynnie.

"How would I know that"? Asked Paul.

"Aren't you one of them"? Asked Wynnie.

"Them"? Asked Paul.

"The aliens", stated Wynnie.

"Aliens? No, I'm not one of them. I came down here because I heard an APB on the police scanner about a missing daughter. I thought there may be a story in it for me, so here I am. Did you really say aliens?" Asked Paul.

"You're human, then"? Questioned Wynnie.

"Since birth", stated Paul.

"Get me out of here", demanded Wynnie.

"I wanted to investigate and get a good story out of all of this", declared Paul.

"No, the aliens kill any man that enters here", exclaimed Wynnie.

"OK, we'll leave here but you have to promise me before I lead you out of here that you'll give me an exclusive interview for my story", replied Paul.

"Anything, just get me out of here", stated Wynnie as she struggled to get on her feet.

Paul led Wynnie back the way he had come. When Wynnie began to speak, Paul put his hand over her mouth and motioned for her to remain very quiet. Paul moved his mouth close to Wynnie's ear and stated, "We have several levels that we need to climb. One of those levels has an entire city built within it. We don't want to be stopped during our exit. If you need to communicate something to me, tug my shirt and I'll hand you my note book and you can write what you need to say down. We don't want to speak and give away our location. Understand"? Asked Paul. Wynnie nodded she understood. Paul removed his hand from her mouth and signaled for Wynnie to follow quietly. Wynnie held onto the back of Paul's shirt as they walked slowly upward.

Paul stopped to take pictures of the underground city. He made certain to turn off his flash before taking the pictures, then he and Wynnie exited through the nearest wall door. When they neared the entrance, Paul signaled for Wynnie to wait. The guard was watching a portable television set. A baseball game was playing. Paul wrote on his noted pad, for Wynnie to follow very closely as they would need to move very quickly to avoid being caught by the guards peripheral vision. The guard pulled out a sandwich and began to unwrap his lunch. Lettuce tumbled to the ground. The guard bent over to pick up the fallen food, and Paul grabbed Wynnie's hand and pulled her past the entrance way. They ducked below the sign that said, "Guided tour patrons, line up here".

The guard began to eat his sandwich while watching the ball game on television. Paul and Wynnie remained in a squatting position as they waddled below the signs and the hedges that lined the entrance way. When they were finally well past the guard and on the grassy area of the entrance, Paul stood up and helped Wynnie into a standing position too. Paul took Wynnie's hand and they ran to his car. Paul opened the passenger door for Wynnie. She got in. Paul put his key in the ignition but placed the car in neutral. He then told Wynnie to steer the car while he pushed. If they could get the car onto the road without starting the motor, they may be able to get away without being noticed. Wynnie slide into the driver's seat. Paul pushed the car and they were soon on the road. Wynnie slide over and Paul got into the driver's seat and started the car.

"As Paul drove, he handed Wynnie his cell phone and told her to call her mother. Wynnie explained that she had been within the cavern when the lights went out. She said she had gotten lost and was found. Mom sounded relieved that Wynnie was now safe, but voiced concern on getting home safely without further problems. Wynnie told her mother that she would call as soon as she could but she needed to get herself together. Wynnie and the man who rescued her were heading to the local police station. Wynnie had decided to tell her mother the entire ordeal in person and not on the telephone. She didn't know how her mother would handle all the details. Wynnie felt badly not sharing all the information with her mother but she didn't want her mom and dad driving across country to retrieve their one and only daughter. She would get home and tell them as she monitored their reactions. This would give her time to find the right words to say.

"I didn't see my car", stated Wynnie,

"I saw one of their men move it", replied Paul.

When Paul and Wynnie arrived at the police station, surprise could be seen on the officer's face when he recognized Wynnie. "We have an ABP out for you young lady. Can you tell me where you've been and how you happened to be with this mug"? Questioned the officer.

Wynnie was escorted into an office in the back. Paul was told he should wait. An hour and a half later, Wynnie returned to the waiting area. "I am so angry. They think I was lying". The chief of police wandered out to where Paul and Wynnie were standing. "I don't know if you are trying to get a story out of this or not. We don't like being used for a hoax and next time, we'll press charges against you both". Then the chief of police turned and walked away.

"Ooh, I'm so angry I could spit fire", stated Wynnie, "They could have at least checked it out. I'm an honest citizen not some crank pot. They had no reason to doubt me".
"Let's go to my paper. We can look in the archives to see if there were any other missing women near the site of the caverns. I'll try to get in touch with an old army buddy of mine. Maybe he can help us too. It seems if we have enemies and the local authorities won't help, the next line of defense is the military", stated Paul.
"It may be a good distraction at that. I can't seem to stop my mind from thinking about those poor women that are still stuck down there. We need to help them and I do need to figure out how I will be able to get home." said Wynnie.
Paul suggested they go to his paper and research. He promised to pay her money for her story. "The money for your information should be enough to get you home", stated Paul.
The drive took only twenty minutes and soon Paul's car was parked in the paper's parking lot. Moments later, Wynnie and he were in the elevator to the files room.
"Hey Jack, mind if we ramble through your files?" asked Paul.
"Are you looking for anything specific?" asked Jack.

"Abductions. History of the caverns in this area. You know, something to kill time until a good story comes along", replied Paul.

"Abductions? If you want to get scared out of your skin, pull up the taped interview from the unknown man", exclaimed Jack.

"The unknown man?" asked Paul.

"He states he was in the military. He won't give us any real information like his name, rank, address, or such but he says he has cancer and he won't live much longer. He wants the world to know the truth of what's out there", stated Jack.

"If he has cancer, what does he have to lose in giving us his identification?" asked Paul.

"He's afraid for his remaining family", replied Jack.

"Sounds really mysterious. I think that should be first on our list", replied Paul.

Paul and Wynnie headed down to the next level to scan through the archives. Paul shows Wynnie how to look up articles and to search the index card files.

"They are paying someone to computerize these and to down load the articles into files but it's really time consuming. The older stuff won't be done for years", stated Paul.

Wynnie began her searching, when she came across an article on the topic about missing children. She found the reference number and headed down aisle after aisle to find the file. She saw a huge worn out box. "Paul, can you help me get this box down?" she asked.

Paul and Wynnie slide the huge box down and carry it to the large table located near the stairs. An old dangling light illuminates the table.

"What are you interested in? Asked Paul.

"There is an article about abducted children", stated Wynnie.

"Let's check this out together, ok?" asked Paul. Wynnie and Paul sat for hours reading articles to each other about a child or sometimes several children that just seemed to disappear.

"I've counted several hundred children that have been reported as missing in these articles we've browsed or read", stated Wynnie.

Paul looked at Wynnie and nodded. They both had the same thought. Were the aliens abducting the children too?

"Before it gets too late, let's ask Jack to show us that tape", stated Paul.

Jack led Paul and Wynnie into a small room. An old projector sat on a table at the back of the room. The projector faced a large white wall.

"Sit, I'll get this thing going and leave you two to your viewing", replied Jack.

The projector hummed to life. A round light first appeared on the white wall. Jack turned the overhead lights off. He moved back to the projector and flipped several switches. A round wheel began to turn and pull a film in front of the light. Sound erupted.

"You can call me Sam. I refuse to give my real name for the safety of my family", stated Sam.

"Go on Sam", stated a faceless voice from behind the camera.

"I was assigned special duty. They brought me out to the desert. There was an underground bunker that one of the government contractors was having trouble with", stated Sam.

"What kind of trouble'? Questioned the voice.

"Equipment damaged. Areas that had been drilled and cleared were filled with rocks and debris. I'm talking huge rocks and dirt that would take a human days to move. It had to be redone. So they had me, along with a few other guys come out to investigate and halt the vandals. So the other guys and I staked out the bunker. One of the guys had a night vision camera. It was close to 0130 when we saw what I can only describe as a human lizard. It walked like a man, but had a huge tail and was extremely tall. Eight feet or more, was my guess. Gold yellow eyes and black scaly skin. One of the fella's thought someone was playing a practical joke. He ran up to that thing and it tore him apart. Just like he was a piece of paper. Tore him in half. The other two guys and I unholstered our weapons. We started shooting. I hit that son of a bitch. He hollered and grabbed a small device from somewhere on his body. It flashed a red light. Nearly fileted one of the guys. So I threw a grenade. It scattered lizard goo everywhere. We hightailed it out of that place.

My commander had us meet with some high officials. Next thing I know, the instillation bunker was blown up. A huge cement lot was built on top. I didn't know if it were the militaries doing or that of the lizards. My philosophy was to bury those damn lizards", exclaimed Sam.

"What happened then"? Asked the voice.

"The other fellas and I were given orders to never speak of what had occurred. We were all relocated to very distant and lonely bases. It was probably two years, maybe a little longer after my discharge that my old commander got in touch with me. He needed a person he could trust. He gave me an envelope packed full of stuff. He said if anything happened to him to mail that envelope to the media", stated Sam.

"When was that"? Asked the voice.

"I can't tell you but I didn't want any trouble to come knocking at my door. I mailed it to one of those big news station. Pictures were published, and the presidential candidate vowed to produce all the secrets associated with those pictures once he was elected. Nothing was ever seen nor heard of regarding those pictures after that, even though the guy won," stated Sam.

"Why do you think that was"? Asked the voice.

"Because our government knows more and they don't want a repeat of what happened when war of the world's first broadcast on the radio", explained Sam

"So what is the reason you came forward now"? Asked the voice.

"Well, I looked in that envelope. I know I shouldn't have but my curious nature got the better of me. There were a lot of photographs. The one picture that really scared me was the one of rows and rows of what looked like individual pods with people in them", exclaimed Sam.

"Pods with people"? Asked the voice.

"They looked like large glass eggs with a grown person in each one. The people all looked the same. Like someone took a cookie cutter and made the same person for each glass pod", stated Sam.

"What did these pod people look like"? Asked the voice.

"Tall, pale skin with shoulder length almost white hair. Their eyes were closed. They were slender but had muscular thighs and biceps. There were rows and rows of them", stated Sam.

"What do you suppose it all means"? Asked the voice.

"To a person like me, an ex-military man, it looks like an army", stated Sam.

"An army"? Questioned the voice.

"Yes, an alien army. What else would explain people with identical characteristics on such a large scale"? Questioned Sam.

"You believe they are aliens"? Asked the voice.

"Human people don't need glass containers for whatever they are using them for", stated Sam.

"Why would our government support something like that"? Asked the voice.

"That is the million dollar question, isn't it?" Questioned Sam.

"Did you find anything else of interest in the envelope"? Asked the voice.

"A picture of a flying saucer", stated Sam.

"A flying saucer"? Questioned the voice.

"Yes sir. It looked like the one in that movie, oh what was the name of that movie?" Asked Sam.

"Can you describe it"? Asked the voice.

"Greyish silver. It looks like someone put an upside down bowl on top of a saucer plate and painted them. There were lights on the bottom. It looked like it could fit six men if they laid side by side in a circle with their head at the center", explained Sam.

"So about fifteen feet wide"? Asked the voice.

"Yes. It was on a tube like base. Make the center about twelve feet tall", described Sam.

"Was there anything else in the picture"? Asked the voice.

"A military man. I think it was a colonel but it was difficult to tell from the photo", stated Sam.

"Can you share anything else you found in the envelope"? Asked the voice.

"There were a lot of classified reports. I didn't read them. To be perfectly honest, I didn't want my finger prints on anything in the envelope", stated Sam.

"Why was that"? Asked the voice.

"They could find out who sent in the envelope", stated Sam.

"Who are they"? Asked the voice. It was then the film ended. The filmed slapped against the moving reel and made Wynnie jump.

"I wonder if they have a second reel", stated Paul.

"Can we look?" Asked Wynnie. Paul and Wynnie left the viewing area and began searching for films. It seemed hours had slipped by. Paul asked Wynnie if she would like to take a break and get some late lunch or early dinner.

"That sounds great. I didn't realize how late it was and I am hungry", replied Wynnie.

"Any preference on where we eat"? Asked Paul.

"I'm embarrassed because I can't even offer to pay. They took all my stuff when they kidnapped me", replied Wynnie.

"Let's go to the family restaurant a few blocks down the street", suggested Paul, "The meal is on the paper".

Soon a bowl of fresh garden greens were placed in front of them. Once the greens were devoured, the bowls were replaced with a warm entrée of meatloaf, mash potatoes with gravy, a serving of green beans, and a homemade roll.

Paul and Wynnie managed to finish their meal. "I'm stuffed", declared Wynnie.

"I can't believe that. I had to help you finish your meatloaf and beans", replied Paul.

"There was way too much food. Three slices of meatloaf, half a plate of potatoes, plus that delicious dinner roll", stated Wynnie.

"Are you up to more research or would you like to walk off this meal"? Asked Paul.

"Let's walk. I need to figure out how I'm going to get home, who I can contact to let them know about those other women who are being held hostage, and how we can protect our planet from those creatures", voiced Wynnie.

Paul looked at Wynnie. She looked distressed. "Can I do anything to help"? Asked Paul.

"I just want to be in an area where I'll be safe in case it gets dark", replied Wynnie.

"What happened that made you fearful of the dark"? Asked Paul.

"I was lead into that cavern after the lights went off. I don't ever want to be in a position like that again", stated Wynnie.

Paul took Wynnie's hands in his. "No one will kidnap you from me. Let's get you to a hotel", stated Paul.

"Thank you for understanding", replied Wynnie.

The cab driver said nothing after the address for the hotel was requested as the destination. Paul paid the driver and escorted Wynnie inside. Paul paid for the room and they walked to the elevator.

"I guess I'll call my folks and see if they can wire me some money. I don't think the money from me sharing my information will be worth much. Once my folks send me some money, I can take a bus home. It would be cheaper than a plane ticket. I still need to contact someone about those other women. Do you think the FBI would listen to me"? Asked Wynnie.

"Let's get to your room and I'll call my old military buddy. We'll see if we can't figure something out together", stated Paul.

Soon Wynnie was slipping off her shoes and curling up in the chair. Paul had called his friend Wally and was waiting for Wally to swing by the hotel after his shift was over. It seemed hours had passed when Wally knocked on the door.

"Hey, Wally, come on in, we need to ask your advice", stated Paul. Wally came in and sat down.

"Must be something big, you never call in favors", replied Wally.

"Wynnie here was abducted by what may be aliens. She was taken down into a cavern that houses an entire city. We need to tell someone who can help rescue more humans that have been captured. Have any idea who we can talk to?" Asked Paul.

"The general would be the one to bring this type of information too", stated Wally.

"Which nationality are these aliens"? Asked Wally.

"These aliens are not from another country but are from another world", stated Paul. Wally's face paled when he heard what Paul had said. "Definitely the general. If you want, I'll drive you over to the base in my jeep", Stated Wally.

Wynnie and Paul were soon sitting in the general's office. "This is of national concern", stated the general, "We will need to keep you sequestered until we get this situation worked out. You both will be assigned a room in one of our finer military rooms, here on the base".

"I need to get home. My parents are worried. I have no clothes. My purse with my driver license, cash, charge cards, and my car were taken when I was abducted", stated Wynnie.

"We'll get you something to wear. You'll be allowed to contact your parents and let them know you are being asked to assist the government. Of course, we will have to keep the information regarding the aliens a secret at this time", stated the general.

"This is like a nightmare. It's like I have no control over my life. First the aliens and now the government. Why can't I leave"? Asked Wynnie.

"Didn't you say there were other women being held against their will"? Questioned the general.

"Yes, I don't know how many", replied Wynnie.

"We will need you to help us retrieve those women", stated the general.

"I…I…. can't go back down there. I just can't", stated Wynnie becoming visibly upset. Paul moved over and put his arm around Wynnie.

"She's been through too much as it is". Stated Paul.

"I think you two should see something. You'll need to come with me", replied the general.

"Can't it wait until tomorrow? Wynnie has been through a lot and is exhausted", stated Paul.

"No, we need to get on this quickly", stated the general as he called for his car. Paul, Wynnie, and the general climbed into the general's car and the car drove through the military base extremely slow. "I don't want you to panic, but I will confide in you. I will share some classified information. You both must vow to never tell another living person about what you are about to see", stated the general.
Wynnie looked at Paul.

The driver of the general's car stopped the car several miles from the general's office. The building they now entered seemed deserted. The general lead Paul and Wynnie into a room. The room was dark and there was one window. Rows of seats were placed so all the seats faced the window. Paul and Wynnie sat in the row of seats in front of the window. Soon a light could be seen on the other side of the window.

An alien walked in and sat at the table in the room. The alien faced the window. The alien sat directly in line with the seat Wynnie was sitting in. Wynnie grabbed Paul's hand. The general stated, "This is a one way mirror. We can see and hear him, but he cannot see or hear us".
A military man turned on a voice recorder and said, "Tell us about you and why you are here".
"We are here to help you. I have told you that my people are protecting your planet from the evil ones. We have been your guardians for centuries. Unfortunately, the evil ones have made a landing on your planet. They killed some of my people. My son was one of those killed. His body was found along with his travel pod at Roswell many decades ago. We know there are humans that know where the evil aliens are living". The alien stood walked to the window, and spoke directly to Wynnie. "You know where they are and must help us".

Wynnie stood and began to run out of the room. Paul stopped her. "I thought he couldn't see us. He did. He knew exactly where I was. He knew", stated Wynnie hysterically.

Paul held Wynnie in his arms and said, "General, I think we need to get her to out of here and to her room".

The general lead Paul and Wynnie to his car. The car slowly drove them back to his office. Paul and Wynnie sat on the sofa in the general's office while the general made arrangements for Paul and Wynnie to stay on base.

The general excused himself. Paul and Wynnie sat on the sofa. Wynnie felt safe in Paul's arms. She hadn't felt safe since this entire ordeal had begun. The general came back into the office. He was followed by the alien. Wynnie screamed.

"There is no need for alarm. I will not harm you. I am a guardian to mankind. I am here to protect you. My name is Ky", stated the Alien.

"You're one of them", yelled Wynnie as she looked around for a way to escape the room.

"No, the other ones are the evil ones. My people are here to protect your race. The evil ones try often to make it into your atmosphere. The ozone layer is dense and difficult to enter. Unfortunately, your citizens have caused a hole in the ozone layer making their arrival easier. I believe you call it global warming. My people attempt to stop the evil ones before they can enter your planet's atmosphere. You may see our sky battles but they look like meteor showers or northern lights from the surface of the earth", stated the alien.

"If you protect us, then how did they manage to get in and abduct all those women and me"? Asked Wynnie.

"They managed to shoot down one of my people's travel pod over Roswell. My son, Kyst, died trying to save your planet. The evil ones discovered they couldn't survive with all the microorganisms that breed on this planet. They have managed to stay here but my fellow clan has not been able to discover where they are located. I believe you know where they live and you can help us", stated the alien.

"I can't help you. I can't go back there. I am sorry for those other women. I am in anguish over having been saved and they are still there, but I just can't go back there", exclaimed Wynnie.

"General, you can't think that this young woman would be able to be of much help. This entire experience has left her anxious, paranoid, as well as afraid of the dark", stated Paul.

The general sat and motioned for KY to take a chair. The large alien managed to sit in a hard wood chair in front of the general's desk. "Wynnie does not have to go anywhere. We were hoping she would guide KY and his group to the women, but it's obvious she would not be able to do that. However; she may be able to draw a map of what she has seen. Where the women are located and how many of the other aliens may be in the area" stated the general.

Paul kept his arms around Wynnie. The general picked up the telephone and called someone. Soon a knock was heard at the door. A soldier was carrying in large sheets of paper and two packages of markers. The general instructed the soldier to place the items on his desk. The soldier obeyed, saluted, turned, and then left the room.

"Ky, why don't we leave these two to be alone to make some maps for us", suggested the general. KY nodded in agreement. The general let KY leave the room first. Before he closed the door, the general said, "I'll have some sandwiches and beverages brought in".

"I know I must seem like a big baby", stated Wynnie, "but the women I met had said that one of the abducted women had tried to escape. The aliens caught her and peeled off the escapee's skin, muscles, and drained her blood while that woman was still alive. They made all the abducted women watch to deter them from trying to escape. I'm afraid. No, not afraid but terrified of going back there".

"Let's draw them the best maps we can. That should be as good as you going there. It would seem to me that the less people that go in, the less likely the group would be of getting caught", stated Paul in attempts of calming Wynnie.

Wynnie and Paul worked on the map. Paul drew the various levels that he had encountered while in the cave. Wynnie drew the layout of the level where the hostages were being housed. Hours later, the general came back. He looked over the maps and nodded his approval.

"Let's get you two a good night's sleep", stated the general. Wynnie looked frightened.

"Will Wynnie and I be on the same floor"? Asked Paul.

"You'll be in the same suite", stated the general. Wynnie took a deep breath.

"That is a good idea", stated Paul.

"Well, I will tell you, we will have one of our shrinks talk to you", the general said to Wynnie.

"To me"? Questioned Wynnie.

"Yes", replied the general," you need to be debriefed on the situation. I think you could also use a little insight into how to resolve this fear issue this event has caused you".

Wynnie nodded that she understood. The general, Paul, and Wynnie again entered the general's car. He drove them to yet another area of the base. The car stopped in front of what could have been an administrative building if it had not housed on the base. The general escorted Paul and Wynnie to the fifth floor. The general opened a set of double doors and said, "This is the suite you will be staying in until we complete this mission".

"Not bad", stated Paul.

"The shrink will come here. You won't have to worry about going out of the building at night. It appears you seem to feel safer with Paul nearby. We will try to accommodate you to the best of our ability", stated the general.

"General, would you be able to get a few things for Wynnie to wear? I can go to my apartment and pick up some of my things, but all her stuff has been lost in this ordeal", stated Paul.

"I'll see to it that you both have the apparel you need. You will not be allowed to leave the facility until our mission has been completed", stated the general.

Wynnie and Paul looked at the general. "How long will that be"? Asked Paul.

"A few days or so", replied the general.

"I need to call my folks", stated Wynnie.

"We will arrange for you to call. You must understand, there will be someone listening on another line to ensure you do not breach this mission. No one is allowed to know about aliens, abductions, or our plan to contain them", stated the general.

"I understand", replied Wynnie.

"We'll set you up to call home at 2000", stated the general.

A knock on the door made Wynnie jump. The general opened the door to find two soldiers escorting another soldier. A female soldier. "Ah, doctor, I'm glad you are here. This is your new patient", stated the general as he pointed to Wynnie. Wynnie gulped and her eyes grew wide.

"No need to be frightened. I am what the general calls a shrink. I am a psychiatrist that has done research in helping people who have come through traumatic events. I hope you'll let me help you too", stated the shrink.

Wynnie nodded yes.

"Why don't we go somewhere private so we can talk", said the shrink.

Wynnie nodded yes and stood.

"I'm Doctor George, but you may call me Sherry", stated the shrink.

"I'm Wynnie", replied Wynnie.

"Have you chosen which room you will be sleeping in"? Asked Sherry.

Paul and Wynnie both replied "No", in unison.

"Why don't we make the bedroom to the right yours and go have a chat in there", suggested Sherry to Wynnie.

Wynnie agreed and they left.

"General, I didn't want to say this in front of Wynnie, but how are you and just a handful of what you call good aliens going to destroy layer after layer of evil aliens"? Questioned Paul.

"We have our ways. We are working out the details and plan on striking soon. We will have to keep you two sequestered until the entire plan has been expedited. Oh, and one other thing, my boy, you will not be able to print any of this in your paper", stated the general.

"You can't stop me from writing a story. Freedom of speech is a constitutional right", replied Paul.

"I'm afraid I can and will. Any word of aliens on this planet may cause harm to the world we know. If you try to publish anything regarding this situation, you could be considered an enemy of the state. I'm afraid enemies of the state have a very poor future", replied the general.

Paul's face turned beet red. He was angry but knew he had to calm down and think before arguing further with the general.

"Oh, in case you have any ideas about leaving, I have posted guards outside your door and positioned them around the building. I want to keep you both and America safe", stated the general as he opened the door to leave.

It seemed like hours had gone by before Wynnie and Doctor George finished talking. Wynnie looked a lot better.

"I'll speak with the general about that matter. Let's plan on me talking to you again in a day or two. We'll see how you feel and if things are better for you, ok"? Questioned the Doctor.

"Ok", replied Wynnie.

The doctor had only been gone for several moments before several soldiers hauled in two huge boxes.

"The general said we were to leave these articles of clothing for you. He said to notify the guard outside if you need anything else", stated the soldier.

Wynnie looked puzzled.

"These boxes must contain the clothing the general said he'd bring to us", stated Paul.

Paul began opening the boxes. He pulled out shirt after shirt of camouflage material. Then he pulled out pants of camouflage material. He found underwear and laughed. "At least it's not camouflage", Paul stated.

Wynnie laughed too. It seemed like she hadn't laughed in a long time. It felt odd to laugh.

"I assume that other box is for you", stated Paul.

Wynnie opened the box to find, kaki colored pants and shirts. She found bras and underwear. There were socks and several pairs of boots. The boots were of various sizes.

"I guess I should have told them my shoe size", replied Wynnie.

"See anything that you need that isn't there", Asked Paul.

"They forgot hair brushes and tooth brushes", replied Wynnie.

Paul opened the door and spoke to the soldiers guarding their new living quarters. The soldier nodded and said, "We'll take care of it".

Paul closed the door, turned and said, "They will get some toothbrushes and hair brushes. He said we can order dinner via the telephone".

"The telephone. Oh, that reminds me, I need to call my mom and dad", stated Wynnie.

Wynnie picked up the telephone and a voice came on line. "How may I assist you"?

"I need to call my parents", replied Wynnie.

"Dialing now, mame'" stated the voice.

Wynnie held her hand over the mouth piece and whispered to Paul, "How did she know the number to my parents when I didn't even tell her who I was"?

"I'm sure the general took care of all the details", replied Paul.

Wynnie's mother answered the telephone on the second ring and said, "Hello".

"Hi Mom, it's me", stated Wynnie.

"Where are you? Are you on your way home"? Asked Wynnie's mother.

"Not yet, I'm afraid. I have been asked to help the local authorities. They will get me home when they believe the work is complete", stated Wynnie.

"You've been through so much already. Do you have any idea when you will be through"? Asked mom.

"Hopefully soon, mom. I want to come home as soon as possible", replied Wynnie.

After eating, Wynnie excused herself and took a long hot shower. After climbing in bed, it was only moments before she fell asleep. Wynnie tossed and turned all night. She kept dreaming of the aliens. She dreamed of the gray creatures that collected the newborn aliens. She dreamed of the tall alien woman who forced women to endure the birthing ritual. And she dreamed of Rudy. Rudy who voiced earth women were of no consequence and whose lives were of no importance to him. Yes, the women who were only captives.

Wynnie awoke when she dreamed of the captive women screaming. Her bed linens were disheveled and damp. It was just beginning to get light outside. She got up and took a hot shower. She tried on the clothes the general had ordered delivered. She had to try on several pairs of boots before she found a good fit. She brushed her hair and teeth then went into the adjoining room. Paul was asleep on one of the sofas.

Wynnie ordered breakfast for her and Paul. Soon a knock was heard at the door. Paul jumped. "I'm sorry, I thought I would order breakfast", stated Wynnie.

The soldier brought in a cart with various breakfast items. The soldier placed the cart in the middle of the room and then left.

The general arrived shortly afterward and asked Wynnie to have a seat. Paul joined them. The general helped himself to a cup of coffee. After taking a large sip of coffee, the general said, "The shrink believes it would help you if you were informed of the outcome of our rescue mission", stated the general.

"I feel so guilty about being free and those other women are still stuck there. I think it would help me if I had some closure", stated Wynnie.

"After giving it some thought, I believe having you at the recovery destination would solve two problems. Your survivor guilt would be resolved and you could offer reassurance to the women we hope to rescue", replied the general.

"Can Paul accompany me"? Asked Wynnie.

"Yes, yes. I assumed he'd go too", stated the general.

"When and how"? Asked Paul.

"I can't share that information with you. However, I can tell you to be ready to go at a moment's notice. I'll have my men pick you up and escort you to the recovery destination at the appropriate time", informed the general.

"It will be today, won't it"? Asked Wynnie.

"Orchestrating a rescue mission takes time. We must gather Intel and strategically plan for any contingency. That's all I can say at this time", replied the general. He gulped down the remainder of his coffee and then left.

Wynnie sat down. Paul could see her hands had formed into tight fists.

"Are you ok"? Asked Paul.

"I'm scared. Really, really scared", stated Wynnie.

Paul sat down beside Wynnie. "You'll be safe at the recovery destination. I think they want you to see the women were rescued so it will put your mind at ease. It will help the women they rescue too", stated Paul.

"How will it help them"? Asked Wynnie

"Seeing someone familiar will help them feel more secure",
answered Paul. Paul placed his hands over Wynnie's hands.
"Thank you for saving me. And thank you for helping me
through all this", stated Wynnie.
"I'm not really a hero. I was in search of a story", replied Paul.
"Well, you saved me all the same. You even stood by me at
my weakest moment", stated Wynnie.
"You looked like you needed a friend", replied Paul.
"I did and you were there. I could never thank you enough",
stated Wynnie.
The day dragged by. Paul kept trying to put a spin on his
story. He kept asking Wynnie question after question.
"I think I need to stop thinking about that place, at lease for a
little while. I need my mind on something else", replied
Wynnie. She stood and gazed out of the window. The day had
dragged on but soon Wynnie decided it was late enough to go
to bed. She excused herself and went into her room.

Paul knocked on Wynnie's door. It was two o'clock in the morning. Wynnie quickly dressed. When Wynnie went into the adjacent room, the general, KY, and KY's team were waiting for Wynnie and Paul.

"You've kept us waiting long enough young lady", stated the general.

"I don't understand", stated Wynnie.

"He's trying to tell you it's time", replied Paul.

Wynnie blanched. Paul held out his hand. Wynnie put her hand in his.

"I'm frightened", exclaimed Wynnie.

"No one will separate us", stated Paul with a smile. Paul could feel Wynnie trembling.

"I have a plan just in case this situation turns sour", whispered Paul to Wynnie.

"What's your plan"? Questioned Wynnie.

"Run like hell", stated Paul.

Wynnie smiled and replied, "When that plan goes into effect, I hope you won't hold me back".

Paul grinned and squeezed Wynnie's hand.

"Let's go", stated Paul.

Soon, Paul and Wynnie were sitting in the general's car, heading toward another part of the base. Paul and Wynnie were escorted into a green colored van. When the back doors opened, Wynnie could see all sorts of tactical gear housed on the walls above the seats. The seats were attached to both sides of the inner walls of the van. KY and his group were already seated inside. The general entered first. Paul followed the general inside still holding fast to Wynnie's hand. The general sat at the head of the row of seats at the opposite side of KY.

Paul instructed Wynnie to sit at the end seat on the right nearest the door. He knew aliens of any sort were causing Wynnie distress.

"No, we will not betray you", stated KY as all four members of the alien group looked at Wynnie.

"I….I never said you would", replied Wynnie

"My people, it is said, are clairvoyant. We can hear your thoughts. It is understandable why you would not trust us. We do look similar to the evil specie that abducted you. We are here to protect you and your people", stated KY.

"I'm sorry if I have offended you. This whole experience has been a nightmare", replied Wynnie.

"We are not capable of dreaming so your reference is not well understood", stated KY.

"She's trying to say this has been the worst thing that has ever happened to her. Something she never thought could possibly occur", clarified Paul.

"Ky and his team here have proven multiple times to be trustworthy. They have helped in many sticky situations that unfortunately I cannot share with you. Classified my dear", replied the general.

The van came to a stop several hundred feet from the road leading to the caverns. The doors opened abruptly startling Wynnie. Paul pulled Wynnie into his arms. Two military men stood just beyond the open doors.

"Everyone is in place, sir", stated the soldier on the right as he looked at the general and saluted.

"Thank-you, captain. Show me where you have set-up your command center", demanded the general. The general left the van followed by KY and his team. The soldier on the left stood in place.

"Were we suppose to follow the general"? Asked Wynnie. Before Paul could answer, the soldier stated, "I am to escort you to the mobile medical unit".

"Where is the mobile medical unit"? Asked Paul.

"Immediately behind this vehicle is the mobile medical unit" stated the soldier.

Paul stood and led Wynnie down from the green van. It was very dark. There were no street lights and the sky was clouded over offering very little illumination. It was so cloudy even the moon and the stars couldn't be seen. The soldier led Paul and Wynnie to the mobile medical vehicle. Once the door was opened, a soft green light glowed offering a guided path to enter.

After the exterior door closed, a second door opened. It took Paul and Wynnie a few moments to get their eyes accustomed to the light change. The lights were quite bright. A team of medical personnel, all wearing scrubs, were readying various types of equipment. A doctor approached Wynnie "Would you be able to give me an idea on what we may see"? Asked the doctor.

"Well, some of the women may be like me. They were using me to harvest my eggs. There are women who are pregnant with alien babies, and some that may have recently delivered", stated Wynnie. Wynnie explained how the women were prepared for more implantations and the yellow goop that had been shoved into her.

"We should probably draw some blood and complete a physical examination on you to ensure you are ok too." stated the doctor.

"Why?" asked Wynnie.

"How did you know they removed your eggs?" asked the doctor.

"Rudy told me what they had done", stated Wynnie.

"You believed him?" asked the doctor.

"Oh, I see your point. Will you let me know if you find anything out of the normal?" asked Wynnie.

"Of course", replied the doctor.

Wynnie looked at Paul for guidance.

"It may make you feel better knowing you haven't been exposed to anything foreign that could harm you", replied Paul.

Wynnie licked her lips and nervously nodded yes. "Follow me", stated the doctor.

Wynnie looked back at Paul as she slowly walked through another set of doors.

An hour later, Wynnie emerged from the examine room in the back of the mobile medical unit. She looked drained. Paul walked to her and put his arm around her shoulder.

"Did the doctor say anything?" asked Paul.

"He found needle marks in the area of my ovaries. He collected some of the chemical they inserted, and he drew some blood. Guess we'll need to wait and see what the results of the tests show", stated Wynnie.

They had just begun to walk back to an area with seats when the front doors opened. Two military men escorted Donna inside. Donna looked more fatigued and extremely frightened. Wynnie walked up to Donna and hugged her. "You are safe now", stated Wynnie. Donna began to weep uncontrollably. Wynnie held her tight and silently stood while Donna drained all the tears from her system. The medical crew moved forward. A nurse put her arm around Donna. "We need to make certain you are alright. Please come with me", instructed the nurse.

Donna turned to Wynnie and said, "thank you for not leaving me there".

Soon the medical unit was very crowded. Six more women had been recovered. Several of the women were those that Wynnie had seen while she was a captive in the cavern. A small alarm like sound was repeating itself as the women entered. The back door had barely closed when five more women were ushered in. Wynnie didn't recognize the second group of women. Several of the women were pregnant. Paul could only stare in disbelief. The mobile medical unit began to move. Wynnie looked frightened.

"Why are we moving? There must be other women down there?" exclaimed Wynnie.

"Maybe this unit can only care for so many and then another mobile medical unit takes the next group of women that are recovered", stated Paul. Wynnie seemed to calm when she heard Paul's explanation. Paul and Wynnie sat while the mobile medical unit relocated. With no windows in the vehicle it was difficult to tell where it may be going.

"I am sorry for being so emotional. I'm not usually like this. I'm not certain why I can't seem to get myself together", replied Wynnie.

"You've been through a really bad ordeal. One that no one else on earth has been through. Of course you are emotional. Who wouldn't be", replied Paul.

The mobile medical unit drove for over an hour. When the mobile unit stopped, doors from the front and back suddenly opened. Medical personnel raced in and assisted to transport all the women into a tall building.

"Mame', will you please follow me?" asked a man in scrubs as he looked at Wynnie.

"Why do I need to follow you?" asked Wynnie.

"General's orders. We need to evaluate anyone who may have gone into the cavern", stated the man.

"Paul and I were both in the cavern", replied Wynnie.

The man looked at Paul. "He needs to come too, but we need to make certain any woman who was in contact with the aliens have not been exposed to alien micropathogens", replied the man.

"Micro what"? Asked Paul.

"Germs", replied the man, "Please, follow me".

Hours later, Paul was sitting in the lobby waiting for Wynnie to be released from the military hospital. He grabbed a cup of coffee and mentally began writing his story. Soon rays of the sun could be seen flickering through the windows. Paul rested his head against the wall and closed his eyes. Soon dreams began.

"Paul, help me. Please Paul, help", Wynnie called. Paul could hear Wynnie but he couldn't see her. They were back in the cavern. He could see aliens leading a line of women into a large room. The women had their hands tied and many were pregnant.

"Your people have attacked us. We will make you all pay for their mistake", replied one of the aliens. The women were placed in the middle of the room. Many of the women were crying. A group of aliens surrounded the women. The leader of the alien group lifted one woman up by the neck. Paul could see her struggling to get free. The woman was fighting to get air. The alien was smiling as he watched the woman struggle more fiercely to try and breathe. She couldn't get any air. The woman finally passed out. The alien just dropped the woman to the ground with a loud thud.

Paul could hear what sounded like a group of children running. Young aliens entered the room. The alien leader said something to the alien children in their language. The young aliens walked up to the women. Suddenly the young aliens began biting the women. They sucked blood from the captives as the women attempted to free themselves of their restraints and move away from the savage abuse. Anguishing screams could be heard. Paul awoke with a start. He was drenched in sweat and could feel his heart racing. He was wiping his face when Wynnie emerged.

"I guess we can go now", replied Wynnie. She took one look at Paul and saw something was wrong. "Are you ok?"

"Just a bad dream", he replied, "I dozed off and dreamed of those damn creatures of yours".

A jeep was running and waiting for Paul and Wynnie. The driver drove them back to their rooms. The general was sitting drinking a tall glass of whiskey. When he saw Wynnie, the general stated, "I'm afraid we were unable to rescue all the women that were abducted".

"I don't understand", stated Wynnie.

"What happened?" asked Paul.

"KY and his men were able to rescue the first batch of women. When they returned to retrieve others, they ran into an evil alien sympathizer. The sympathizer set off an alarm of some kind. KY, his men, and the women they had with them managed to get out before the entrance was barricaded by rubble from some type of blast", explained the general.

"How can you be sure the evil aliens can't get out?" asked Wynnie.

"KY and his men placed some canisters with lethal gas inside the cavern. It was released when KY realized the rescue efforts were over", stated the general.

Paul and Wynnie didn't know what to say.

Wynnie turned to Paul and said, "Had someone else run into you that day, I may be dead and my body lying within the cavern".

Paul took Wynnie into his arms. He hugged her tightly.

"Don't beat yourself up. Military personal have to anticipate collateral damage", replied Paul.

"What is collateral damage?" asked Wynnie.

"When some local or in this case, some of our own people get harmed in the process of winning the war", explained Paul.

The general finished his drink and said, "I'll be in touch". The general left abruptly.

Wynnie stood and walked to her room. She closed the door.

Paul knocked on Wynnie's door. "Can I come in?" asked Paul.

"I'm tired, Paul. Really, really tired", replied Wynnie as she wiped the tears that were streaming down her face.

"I think we need to get some food into you then you can do some serious sleeping", replied Paul.

"I don't feel up to eating anything", replied Wynnie.

"Then I'll order something light", replied Paul.

Wynnie came out of her room. "Is it wrong to feel glad I'm alive when the other women are dead?" asked Wynnie.

"Not at all. It is wrong to blame yourself because some of the women didn't make it out. It was the alien sympathizer who prevented the others from being rescued", stated Paul.

"I just can't shake this feeling, that I could have died", replied Wynnie.

"Think of how your parents would have felt if you hadn't made it out. The other women went missing a while ago. Their families have already grieved for them and most likely have moved on, accepting their deaths", stated Paul.

A tray of food was delivered. Wynnie nibbled on some fresh fruit and had a cup of tea. Paul ate a couple sandwiches and had coffee. Wynnie stood, said, "good night", and walked to her room, closing the door behind her.

Paul could hear voices coming from Wynnie's room.

"I just wanted to hear your voice. I missed you, mom. I wish I was home", stated Wynnie.

"I wish you were home too, honey. Can you tell me why you sound so down?" asked Mom.

"I can't yet", replied Wynnie.

"Do you know when you'll be able to come home?" asked mom.

"Not yet. There is still some information that I need to offer the authorities", replied Wynnie.

"That's understandable. We wouldn't want any other women to get lost if they can figure out what happened and fix the problem. I can't tell you what I went through when you went missing. I'm so glad you are safe", stated mom.

"Thanks mom. I needed to hear that", replied Wynnie.

"You know we love you", stated mom.

"I know. I love you too", replied Wynnie.

"I'm glad you called. I really miss you", stated mom.

"I miss you too", replied Wynnie catching a sob in her throat.

"Ok, honey. Call and let me know when we can expect you", instructed mom.

"I will. I promise", replied Wynnie.

Wynnie went to bed and slept. She slept through lunch and woke up around three in the afternoon. After her shower, she went into the living area. Paul was a sleep on the sofa. Wynnie went back to her room and ordered dinner for her and Paul. When dinner arrived, Paul jumped. "What happened?" asked Paul.

"Dinner", replied Wynnie.

Again the waiter remained silent. The waiter left and ten minutes later, the general knocked.

"I thought you may want an update", stated the general.

Wynnie and Paul sat quietly.

"Eleven of the women survived. Sadly, when the women that were pregnant were examined, the yellow colored gelatin substance was displaced. The creatures inside the women went wild and began tearing and ripping themselves free of their hosts. The women bled to death", explained the general.

"She didn't need to hear that", shouted Paul.

"I think she did. She needs to know how those creatures needed to be destroyed. She has already seen how little regard they have for human life. She and the other women are lucky to be alive. We all are lucky the evil ones are destroyed", stated the general.

"How do you know they are destroyed?" asked Wynnie.

"Ky took care of that. He and his group planted chemicals along the paths. Once those chemicals are detonated, it will destroy everything in the cavern. That poisonous gas will ensure all the evil ones are destroyed", stated the general.

"It must have been awful for the women!" stated Wynnie. Paul just shook his head. "It seems there could have been a way to rescue the women. A swat team", suggested Paul.

"The evil aliens have a good sense of smell. The can pick up on testosterone", stated the general.

"Why didn't they catch me?" asked Paul.

"It seems they have several human men or should I say had, working for them", replied the general.

"I don't understand why anyone would work with them", stated Wynnie.

"They held their female family members hostage. Threatened to kill them unless they helped them", explained the general.

"How awful", stated Wynnie.

"So now what?" asked Paul?

"That is the question. I'm afraid this situation is classified. I need you both to understand the government will use whatever means to squelch this information. That means you two must never tell a soul about any of it. Wynnie, your story is you were lost in the cavern, along with others in your tour group. One of the men in your group would not let anyone wander off. You felt kidnapped and attempted to leave the group when the opportunity arose. Paul found you and took you to the police station. Paul, you can report on the unstable rock structures of the cavern and its collapse", instructed the general.

"That could harm ticket sales at other caverns", stated Paul.

"Then find a story that will say the cavern collapsed. A terrorist, kids playing with dynamite, something", stated the general.

"Does that mean I can go home?" asked Wynnie.

"I've arranged a flight for tomorrow. I just wanted to make certain you recognize the seriousness of this situation", stated the general.

"I understand. Will I still be able to get the results from my blood tests?" asked Wynnie.

"No. All information regarding this situation is classified. Are we done here?" asked the general.

"Yes, I just want to go home", replied Wynnie sadly.

"You won't have any trouble from us", exclaimed Paul.

"Good to know. You'll receive your travel itinerary tomorrow at breakfast. You'll also get a new outfit. No military gear leaves this hotel". The general grabbed his hat and left.

"Well, I guess tonight is the last night we'll get to spend together", said Wynnie sadly.

"Let's eat and savor our time together", suggested Paul.
Paul and Wynnie stayed up late talking about their experiences and how each would deal with the aftermath.
"You know, I'm a writer, but I have no idea what it is that you do", stated Paul.
"I teach", replied Wynnie.
"You are a school teacher? That explains why you visited the cavern. They say experience allows better teaching", stated Paul.
"Actually, I teach online at the college level. I just landed the job right out of college. I got really lucky. On line teaching positions are difficult to find", replied Wynnie.
"What subject do you teach?" asked Paul.
"Writing", replied Wynnie.
"And you teach from home?" inquired Paul.
"Yes. It can be tedious sitting in front of the computer all day. But I can work in my pajamas", smiled Wynnie.
"I wish I could work in pajamas. I'm lucky sometimes if I get to shower and change clothes every day", replied Paul.
"So how do you get your stories? Do people call the paper or do you find the stories yourself?" asked Wynnie.
"Both actually. People call in when they see something newsworthy and sometimes we come across a story or topic we'd like to do", explained Paul.
"Too bad you can't write the real story. I think the world is more receptive to things than they were years ago", stated Wynnie.
"We tell people of war all the time. It's not like it's something new", replied Paul.
"Well, people fear what they don't know", replied Wynnie with a yawn.
"I guess we should get to bed. It is rather late", said Paul.
"I am sleepy", admitted Wynnie. She stood and waved good night.

Morning came too soon. An outfit was delivered at 0500 for Wynnie. She had only slept two hours after going to bed at 2:30 a.m. Wynnie showered and dressed. She had nothing more with her. Her belongings were in her car. She had no idea where her car had been taken or if it would ever be found. Her purse, wallet, money, and identification must now be buried under tons of rubble.

Wynnie entered the living area to find a tray of coffee and breakfast entrées.

"I'm on my third cup", stated Paul holding his coffee cup up.

"Didn't you go to bed last night?" asked Wynnie.

"I tried, but my mind wouldn't stop working on my story line", replied Paul.

"I hate when I can't shut my thought processes off", replied Wynnie reaching for a coffee cup.

"I have been trying to clear my head, but the ideas keep racing through my mind. I wish I weren't restricted. This would make a great story", stated Paul.

Wynnie picked up a cup and filled it with coffee and said, "I thought I'd have my itinerary by now. You didn't see it on the tray did you?"

"I'll call Wally and see if he can get it for you", stated Paul. Paul picked up the telephone and asked for Wally's number to be dialed. Soon Paul heard Wally's voice on the other end of the line. "Hey Wally. The general told Wynnie he would send her an itinerary for her route home. She wanted to let her folks know when to expect her. Her clothes arrived but not her itinerary. Can you see if the general has sent it over yet?" asked Paul.

"I'll check with the general and get back with you", stated Wally.

Wally hung up the telephone and walked into the office of the general's secretary. The secretary was not in her office. Wally walked over to knock on the general's door but heard the general voice. "The general must be talking to someone", Wally said to himself. Wally didn't want to interrupt and waited for the general to finish his conversation.

"I believe we fooled them. KY and his team believe they destroyed your lair. I had the poison gas containers filled with helium and dye. KY and his men believed it would kill you. With that said, when can I expect the next payment from your people?" asked the general.

Wally couldn't believe his ears. He quietly left the office. He raced to his jeep and took off. When Paul heard the knock on the door, he was surprised to see Wally.

"I thought you would you call us with the itinerary", stated Paul.

"I never got that far. I think we need to talk", stated Wally. Then looking at Wynnie and added, "Alone".

"Ok", replied Paul with a puzzled look on his face.

"Let's take a little drive", suggested Wally.

Paul looked at Wynnie and then asked Wally, "Will we be back by two o'clock?"

"I'm not sure", replied Wally anxiously.

"Wynnie, please let me know when you get home. I would really like to keep in touch if you think you may be up to it", replied Paul. Paul gave Wynnie one of his business cards and then hugged her tightly. The hug lasted for a long time.

"It's hard to believe this ordeal is almost over", stated Wynnie.

"We'll have the guards contact the general for your flight plan so you'll be able to let your folks know when to expect you", stated Wally. Wally then tapped Paul on the arm and said, "come on, we need to go".

After they climbed into Wally's jeep, Paul stated, "I was hoping to spend as much time as I could with Wynnie before she left. What is going on that is so urgent?"

"The evil aliens are still alive. The general is actually helping them", stated Wally.

"What?" exclaimed Paul?

"I overheard the general. He was talking to one of them", explained Wally.

"How did you overhear them?" asked Paul.

"I was out in his secretary's office. The secretary was out of the office. I went to knock on the general's door and overheard him speaking about fooling KY and his team.

"Let me think. Do you know how to get a hold of KY?" asked Paul.

"Sort of", replied Wally.

"What do you mean, sort of? We need to get in touch with someone who can do something about this situation. The only one who comes to mind is KY", stated Paul.

"We usually go to this small coffee shop. We call a number that is penciled in on the wall. Someone tells us where to meet KY", replied Wally.

Ten minutes later, Wally dialed the number and was told where he could meet with KY. Wally drove to a specific road in a small nearby city. Wally and Paul exited the vehicle and walked down a vacant alley. Wally stopped at a dark brown door and knocked loudly. When the door opened, KY was standing there.

"Please enter", instructed KY.

Wally and Paul walked into the building. The building was a large warehouse. The lightening was very dim. Only the sunlight from outside of the warehouse managed to shine through the windows at the top of the building gave shadowy lights to the floor below. KY walked through the darkened aisles with ease. It appeared as though his eyes could see well in the dark. Wally and Paul were having difficulty navigating down the same aisles. They often stepped on an item or almost tripped over articles that were stacked in the walkway.

KY led Wally and Paul into an office. There were crates and barrels but no furniture. KY sat on a barrel and signaled Wally and Paul to sit. Wally and Paul managed to find a crate to sit on while speaking with KY.

"KY, I overheard the general speaking to an evil alien. He fooled us into believing they were destroyed. He must have warned them we were coming. I also overheard that he had fooled you into believing you place poisonous gas in barrels in the cavern. The general replaced the poisonous gas with helium and some type of colored dye to make it appear like poison", stated Wally.

"My people are unable to pick up everyone's thoughts. The general is one of those people whom we cannot read", stated KY. KY looked around and asked, "Where is your friend?"

"Which friend" asked Wally?

"Your female friend", KY asked Paul.

"She is flying home today", stated Paul.

"We must go", KY stated as he sat and thought. Suddenly one of KY's men came in.

"We need to go to the airport", stated KY.

"I don't understand", stated Paul

"If the general has made arrangements for a flight, he has something else planned", stated KY.

KY led Wally and Paul to a military truck. KY opened the driver's door and handed Wally the keys to the ignition. "You will need to drive", instructed KY to Wally.

The drive seemed like it took forever. Soon they arrived at the military airport. Wally showed his identification to the guard at the entrance and was flagged in. Wally drove the truck toward the airplane hangars.

"They haven't loaded the plane yet", stated Wally, "we can see what the general is planning to ship if we can find the flight plan and manifest".

KY and his men began moving crates off the truck and replaced several of the crates listed on the manifest with those from the truck".

Paul saw the general's car stop and Wynnie got out. A soldier also climbed out to escort Wynnie onto the plane. Once on board, the soldier returned to the general's car and the car immediately took off for its next destination. KY seemed to smile when the flight crew began loading the freight onto the plane. It made Paul uneasy. Paul went on board the plane and brought Wynnie off.

"I thought I wouldn't get to see you before I left", stated Wynnie with a look of relief on her face.

"You need to come with me", stated Paul as he took Wynnie's hand in his and led her off the plane.

"But, I need to get home", stated Wynnie with a confused look on her face.

"Something is going on, but I don't know the specifics of it yet. Please wait and take a different flight", pleaded Paul. Paul continued to lead Wynnie into the hangar.

"You really do believe something is wrong, don't you? What is it that Wally said to you? He knew something this morning, didn't he?" asked Wynnie.

"The general has been working with the evil aliens. He pre-warned them before KY and his men went into the caverns", explained Paul.

"Oh my God. That means they are still able to abuse more women", replied Wynnie. Paul could see the worried look on Wynnie's face. Wynnie looked stunned. Paul guided Wynnie into the back of the truck. KY and his men had also climbed in the back of the truck. Wally climbed into the driver seat and soon had the truck heading toward the warehouse.

The group had been driving for approximately thirty minutes. The silence brought tension. Wally turned on the radio. A news flash was being announced. At 2:15 p.m. a military plane had just reached 2500 feet when it exploded. The newscaster stated that everyone on board was killed. The cause of the explosion was yet to be determined.

The color in Wynnie's face drained from pink to very pale. "I could be one of those dead right now if you hadn't come for me", stated Wynnie to Paul.

"Try not to think about that. Right now we need to focus on the evil aliens. We need to figure out how to defeat them", stated Paul.

Wally, Paul, and Wynnie followed KY into the warehouse. KY turns to them and says, "A battle is going to occur. We have had problems with them for centuries and this must be our last battle".

"For centuries", questioned Wynnie? Just how old are you?"

"Age is of no consequence. The evil ones use to be members of our colony. That was eons ago. They became unsatisfied and greedy. They began to challenge our peaceful leaders. The leaders gave them a choice. They could remain within our civilization and comply or they would be banished to the planet Asphalton", explained KY.

"Did they comply or go to the planet Asphalton" asked Wynnie?

"They went to the planet Asphalton. Unfortunately, their stay on Asphalton was short. They overtook a ship that had arrived with supplies. The evil one and his followers had planned a journey through space. They were seeking a more desirable planet to live on. Unfortunately, they discovered Earth", explained KY.

"How did you and your group happen to come here if the evil aliens were on a different planet", asked Wynnie?

"During the routine surveillance of the planet Asphalton, our leadership council discovered only a sparse group of evil ones on the planet. It was then the collective knew that the majority of the evil ones had escaped", stated KY.

"Then what happened" asked Wynnie?

"After further investigation, it was discovered that the majority of the evil ones had scattered throughout space. Their plan was to find a suitable planet that they could inhabit. They would then send a signal with the coordinates of the newly discovered planet to their other members", stated KY.

"That means there are more evil aliens that may come here? They could pick up the signal and the coordinates?" stated Wynnie.

"My people intercepted one of those signals. The leadership council decided to send groups, like myself to eradicate the planets of any evil aliens present. My group would then be monitors of the assigned planet to ensure no further invasions could occur", stated KY.

"If that is the case, then how is it, the evil aliens are here and have been kidnapping women" asked Wynnie?

"Because the evil ones expected my people to come, they shot down one of my team's pod as they entered the Earth's atmosphere. The space pod shattered and was scattered for miles over Roswell. The pods of my other groups entered from the northern and southern most areas of your planet. We began searching systematically from those points. When we discovered any evil ones, we tried to capture them. We discovered it was not in your population's best interest to attempt to contain them. Some evil ones could control the minds of humans. They would make the human help them escape. Then they would kill and eat the human", explained KY.

"That is awful", replied Wynnie.

"Although my people are peace loving, the council decided it was in everyone's best interest to destroy all the evil ones. Thus destroying the evil aliens has become my objective. Unfortunately, your race must play a key role in the war now too", stated KY.

Wynnie and Paul looked somewhat somnolent.

"Will everyone in the world be involved in this war" asked Wynnie?

"No, your species have very frail members. Only those strong enough will be given the necessary information to fight", instructed KY.

"How do you determine a person is strong enough", asked Paul?

"Humans like yourself. Your armed forces and those armed forces around the world", explained KY. Wynnie leaned into Paul. Paul held Wynnie tight.

"I'm afraid", stated Wynnie.

"It may not be as bad as we think it is", replied Paul.

"We don't know what we are facing until we find out where they have built their city", stated KY.

"What do you mean" asked Paul, "You had to have seen their city when you went to rescue those women".

"We followed your map. There were no cities marked on the maps you drew", stated KY.

"I drew the city on my map" stated Paul.

"The general was able to view those maps before he gave them to KY and his group, didn't he", asked Wally?

"The general. He altered my map so you had no idea about the city", stated Paul, "that can be the only explanation.

"I must take this information to my superiors", stated Wally, "but I'll have to bypass the general. The general must now be considered an enemy of the state".

"I still can't see how you wouldn't be able to see the city from the paths that you were on. I saw them clearly. Matter of fact, I even took pictures of it. If I had my camera here, I could show you the city and how large it was" stated Paul.

"Why couldn't Ky and his men see the city", asked Wynnie?

"Apparently, KY, T, and his group were fooled into believing there were only a small party in the cavern. We saw a city. It's there. How fast can they relocate, do you think" Paul asked KY?

"My species are very strong. It would not take long for a dozen alien men to build walls of stone to block the view of a city. Now we must go back to the cavern and ensure the city is destroyed", stated KY.

"What can we do to help?" asked Paul.

"Wally will contact his superiors and notify them of this situation. You may help us by driving the truck to the cavern. You are wearing military clothing and will look appropriate behind the wheel of a military vehicle. I or my team would look out of place. We must not be stopped", exclaimed KY.

"Well, you can't leave me here alone", stated Wynnie.

"It may be better if you stayed here at the warehouse. I am not certain how dangerous this excursion will be. I don't want to see you harmed", stated Paul.

"She will need to go with us. In the event something happens to you, she has knowledge of the city as well", replied KY. KY then turned and spoke to his team in a language Paul and Wynnie did not understand.

"Let us head to the caverns", instructed KY.

Paul climbs behind the wheel and soon the motor roars to life. Wynnie is escorted into the back of the truck by Lyk, one of KY's team members. Wynnie notices there are a lot of crates inside the back of the truck.

"Where should I sit?" asked Wynnie.

"Nearest the front of the vehicle", states KY.

Wynnie maneuvered through the stacks of crates to the front of the truck. There was a tarp blocking the back storage area from the driving area. Wynnie moved the tarp slightly and saw Paul in the driver's seat.

"I'm glad I can sit near you", replied Wynnie.

"I'm glad too. I need to know you are safe", stated Paul.

After driving for about 45 minutes, KY told Paul to turn down a very small path. The path looked like a tractor path for a farmer. Overgrown weeds and brush easily hid the truck. When KY finally told Paul to stop the truck, KY and his team got out. KY and his group opened the back of the truck. Paul helps Wynnie out.

"What happens now?" asked Wynnie.

"We need to surprise the evil ones. We need you to stay here and be ready to flee. Have the truck turned around and ready to go", instructed KY. KY and three of his team members grabbed two crates each from the back of the truck. They looked at each other and walked in the direction of the cavern.

"Well, you heard him. We need to turn the truck around", said Paul.

Wynnie nodded that she understood as she continued to watch KY and his men disappear into the overgrowth of weeds. When Wynnie heard the truck motor kick to life, she raced to the cab of the truck and climbed into the passenger seat. Time passed slowly. The sun was setting and night slowly arriving across the sky. It was cool and dark when KY and his team returned. As the sky darkened, there appeared several areas that seemed to glow blue in the distance.

"That's odd", stated Wynnie.

"What" asked Paul?

"Look. Those lighted areas seem to be slowly moving our way. How is that possible?" asked Wynnie.

"The evil ones breed drones to fight in this battle", stated KY as he neared the truck.

"Those blue lights are drones" asked Wynnie?

"The evil ones have used a formula that produced Cherenkov radiation", explained KY.

"What is Cherenkov radiation" asked Wynnie?

"It is a process in which subatomic particles shoot off. The particles move faster than the speed of light when in the air which results in a blue glow", stated KY.

"What can these drones actually do" asked Paul?

"They are radioactive. They can burn humans that get too close", replied KY.

"How close is too close" asked Wynnie?

"From a distance of less than ten feet the human body can become poisoned from radiation. If the drones touch a human, the human's skin will blister as if the human was placed on a hot grill", stated KY.

"Shouldn't we get moving then" asked Paul?

"It looks like they are heading this way", exclaimed Wynnie.

"Perhaps it is wise to move you two away from the drones. My people are not affected by radiation" replied KY.

KY and his men removed the remaining crates from the truck. KY then walked up to Paul and said, "Contact your government. Let them know my team will be on the front line of this war. Inform them that the evil ones are using radiation. They will need to bring the weapons my people have given the humans the schematics to build those weapons."

Paul and Wynnie watched KY and his team lug the crates toward the cavern as they drove down the tractor path.

"Where should we go? Do you have any clue where Wally may have gone or who he may have contacted" asked Wynnie?

"Nope, but my friend at the paper may have a clue who we can get in touch with", stated Paul.

"Your friend? Is he military" asked Wynnie?

"No, but he seems to have a ton of connections", replied Paul.

"What is that" asked Wynnie pointing ahead?

"Looks like a road block", replied Paul. Paul slowed the truck down.

"It's the military", squealed Wynnie with relief.

"Sir, you'll need to explain why you are in a military zone", commanded the soldier guarding the barricaded road.

"A military zone? This is the road to the caverns. When did it become a military zone" questioned Paul.

"I'll need to take you two to my commander", stated the soldier.

"We need to speak to whoever is in charge", stated Paul.
"Park the truck over there", instructed the soldier as he
pointed to an area that had other vehicles parked. Paul pulled
the truck into the field and stopped the engine.

"Leave your keys in the vehicle", stated the soldier.

Wynnie looked at Paul and asked the soldier, "Why do we
have to leave the keys"?

"In case they have to move it, I guess", stated Paul. The
soldier nodded in agreement.

Wynnie and Paul climbed out of the truck. "Oh, I forgot my
wallet", stated Paul as he climbed back into the truck for a
brief moment. After Paul climbed out, the soldier stated,
"Follow me".

Wynnie gasped when she saw who was in charge. The general. The general who was helping the evil aliens. The general who would have seen her dead in the plan crash. The general who was an enemy of the state. The general seemed equally surprised to see Wynnie.

"It seems you somehow escaped the unfortunate plane crash", stated the general.

"Why did you cause the plane to crash" asked Wynnie in an angry tone?

"Your friend, KY, caused that plane to explode", stated the general.

Wynnie paled. "KY and his team are here to help us, not to harm us", Wynnie defended.

"Believe what you will, my dear, but it's true", said the general.

Paul pulled Wynnie close and said, "So why were we stopped"?

"Do I look stupid to you, son"? Asked the general.

"I don't follow", replied Paul.

"I know you have knowledge of my connections with the aliens in the cavern. Where is your friend" asked the general?

"What friend would that be?" answered Paul.

"Your little army buddy. The guards at your hotel told me he came for you. Now", yelled the general", where the hell is he"?

"We have no clue" stated Paul as he stood by Wynnie.

"Well, until you remember that information, I'm afraid I'll have to detain you both", stated the general.

Wynnie looked at the general and said, "I don't understand why you feel the need to hold us. I just want to go home".

"This conversation is over", stated the general. The general nodded to the two soldiers that stood by guarding Paul and Wynnie. The two soldiers presented arms and guided Wynnie and Paul from the general's tent and down a row of tents. They escorted Wynnie and Paul several hundred yard away from their truck. They opened the flap of a tent and said, "Let us know when you are ready to talk. We will escort you back to the general". The guards closed and secured the flap.

The tent had a light, a table, several chairs, and two cots. There was only one way in and one way out of the tent, through the flap. Wynnie sat on one of the cots.

"How long do you think they will keep us here" asked Wynnie?

"Not very long, if I have my way", stated Paul.

"What do you mean" questioned Wynnie.

"We know those drones are heading this way. We need to get out of here and get some help", stated Paul, "I'm just not sure how we are going to accomplish that".

Wynnie and Paul sat quietly. Each thinking and attempting to come up with an escape plan. A small scratching sound from the back of the tent drew Wynnie's and Paul's attention. The small hole grew into a larger one. Wally's face came into view. Wynnie and Paul stood. Wally continued to make the opening larger. Wally put his finger to his mouth to signal to Wynnie and Paul to stay quiet. Wynnie and Paul nodded they understood.

Wally helped Wynnie squeeze through the opening first, then helped Paul. Wally led Wynnie and Paul through the tall foliage behind the tent. Wally's trail through the brush went straight, then left, then straight again. They soon came to Wally's jeep. They all climbed in. It appeared that they had escaped without detection.

Wally drove through the field away from the general's camp with the jeep's lights off. Wally followed his previous route with great skill.

"Where are we going" questioned Paul?

"I spoke with my superiors. They realize the general is a turn coat. He managed to escape before my superiors could capture him. I was ordered to take you to safety and then report back to my superiors", explained Wally.

"KY told us to tell you to have your superiors to bring the weapons that KY and his people had given our government the plans to produce", stated Paul.

"Tell him about the drones", stated Wynnie.

"Drones"? Questioned Wally.

"Yes, radioactive drones created to destroy humans", explained Paul.

Wally came to a road and turned left. "He would have had to turn right to get to the military base", thought Paul. Wally drove for about an hour, then pulled the jeep into a parking structure. He parked in the back of the structure, furthest away from the road. Wally got out and signaled for Wynnie and Paul to follow him. Wally led Wynnie and Paul into an elevator and pushed down. When the elevator began its descent, Wally punched the floor buttons, five, three, five, two, and five. The elevator continued below the ground level. Wynnie and Paul looked puzzled as the elevator continued downward.

When the elevator stopped and the doors opened, two guards were guarding a very bright hallway. Wally saluted and led Wynnie and Paul down the long corridor. Wally walked past numerous doors. He suddenly stopped and knocked on what looked like a random door. A voice from the other side of the door stated, "Enter".

Wally entered the room followed by Wynnie and Paul. "General, this is Wynnie and Paul. Wynnie and Paul, this is general Wirwicz", stated Wally.

"Wynnie and Paul, please sit. Wally at ease. I understand you all have been in some way a victim of General McMurrer. Wynnie, I understand you are lucky to be here today", spoke the General Wirwicz.

"Paul talked me into taking a later flight. If he hadn't, I would have been killed in that explosion", explained Wynnie.

"General McMurrer had planned to deviate that flight to an isolated air field. He also had two women who were pregnant with alien babies on board that plane. General McMurrer had every intention of giving you all back to the evil aliens", exclaimed General Wirwicz.

Wynnie felt her stomach roll and said "I'm going to be sick".

Wally moved the trash can near Wynnie. Paul stood and asked, "Is there a restroom nearby"?

The general hit a button on his desk. Soon a man entered the room.

"General", replied the man.

"Doctor, we have an ill woman here. Can you help her"? Asked the General.

"Yes, sir", the doctor replied. The doctor left and moments later came back with a syringe filled with a clear fluid. The doctor walked up to Wynnie and said, "This is Zofran. It will help settle your stomach. It's an injection which means I'll need to access your arm or your hip".

"Let me help" stated Paul as he began rolling up Wynnie's sleeve.

The doctor cleaned Wynnie's arm with an alcohol swipe and with skilled aim and dexterity, gave Wynnie the shot.

"Is there somewhere this young lady can lie down"? Asked the doctor.

The general called someone and soon a wheel chair appeared. Wynnie was assisted into the wheel chair and taken to a room further down the hall.

"Men, we have a problem. We have a rogue general. He knows how the military works and will know how to defend against our efforts", stated the general.

"General, KY gave Paul a message for you" stated Wally.

"KY said to bring the weapons he gave you the blue prints for", replied Paul.

The general made another call. Noises could be heard in the hallway.

"The evil aliens also created radioactive drones to destroy humans. The general knew they had a city in that cavern but hid that fact from KY. KY and his team said to tell you that he and his team are on the front lines", continued Paul.

"We need your help, Paul. You have been in the cavern. You know where the city is or was. We need someone who has accurate information to direct our efforts", stated the General.

"I'm a report, not a soldier", replied Paul.

"We know that, but you play a very important role in this war. You've been where we need to go", stated the general.

"Now I know how Wynnie felt. You do realize, there is the general and drones preventing us from getting near that cavern", stated Paul.

"Show me", stated the General as he pushed yet another button on his desk. A panel on the wall slid downward exposing a large map focusing on the area of the cavern and its surrounding area.

Paul walked up to the map and pointed. "The general has a camp about here, isn't that right Wally"?

"Yes, it's about five miles from the crossroads. The general's command center is here, with surrounding tents and vehicles parked at the ready" stated Wally.

"Drones were here and moving in this direction. I have no idea how the drones communicate with the evil aliens or what their primary objective are", stated Paul.

"Are there any civilians in the area at risk of injury"? Asked the General.

"I'm not that familiar with the area" replied Paul.

"Sir, most of the surrounding area is farmland. I'm not certain how close to the caverns the farm houses may be or how many families may live on the farms", stated Wally.

The general picks up the telephone and spoke to the person on the other end of the connection, "We are going to need a lot of men in hazmat uniforms and field medics able to deal with radiation injuries. Have them ready within 30 minutes".

The doctor knocked and entered the general's office. "Wynnie is resting comfortably. The medication worked well".

"Wally, I'll need you to get Paul set up with combat gear. He'll need to be briefed on the weapons and ready to roll in 30 minutes. Doctor, I need you to assign someone to look after the girl while we are out", instructed the general.

"General, Wynnie has been through a horrific experience. You can't leave her here. She has been with Paul since he found her in the cavern. I don't think she'll agree to stay", stated Wally. "She is too fragile. There are no places to lie down and rest if you feel sick. Unfortunately, I can't send her home yet. We need to debrief her. Right now my men are needed elsewhere", stated the general.

"I think we should give her the option to choose", stated Paul. The general touched and released, touched and released his right index finger tip to his left index finger tip over and over while he mulled over the idea of Wynnie going with Paul and Wally. "Civilians can be risky business," state the general. "It's not her fault she got stuck in the middle of this", defended Paul.

"No one is saying it was. You saw her reaction to the plane situation. We can't stop and call a doctor if she swoons out in the field", exclaimed the general.

"She has been through a lot without swooning. I think we should let her make the decision", stated Paul.

 Ok, we will give her the choice to stay or go, but we must make it clear there is no turning back if she decides not to stay here in safety", stated the general as he pushed a button on his desk. Shortly thereafter a soldier came into the room and said, "Sir, you called?"

"Check on the woman in room 24. See if she is up to coming back to our meeting", instructed the general.

Ten minutes later, a knock was heard on the door. "Enter", yelled the general.

"The gentleman said you wanted to see me", stated Wynnie.

"Wynnie, the general has asked Wally and me to help him. They need someone who has been down inside the cavern. I agreed to go and guide them. I don't think I'll have to go into the caverns but I do need to be nearby so I can offer insight into the pathways and such. You have a choice. You can stay here in this bunker and be safe or you can come with Wally and me" explained Paul.

"That isn't much of a choice", replied Wynnie.

"It's the only one I can offer you at the moment. My suggestion was for you to stay here and wait for us to return. You can be debriefed and then we can make better choices of how to proceed with you leaving after the debriefing", stated the general.

"I don't like the idea of being locked away down here. I have no way to get out if I wanted to. I'd rather go with Wally and Paul", stated Wynnie.

"You must understand, we cannot be slowed down. If you feel ill or scared, we will still have to push onward", stated the general.

"I'll be right beside you", exclaimed Paul as he offered Wynnie a chair.

"It's so difficult to believe that one of our own people would betray us", stated Wynnie.

"Greed affects everyone differently. It's been known to even strike as high as the President of the United States", said Paul.

"We are getting off topic. You'll be given some nourishment and drink. We need to outfit Paul and Wynnie so you can move more easily", explained the general.

"Guess I'll be in combat boots again", said Wynnie with a sad smile.

"Come with me and I'll hook you up", stated Wally. Paul and Wynnie followed Wally. Soon Paul and Wynnie looked military ready. There was a lot of movement near the elevator.

"Where did all those men come from" asked Wynnie?

"This is an underground bunker. It can house hundreds of people for months", explained Wally.

"Where should we go "asked Paul?

"The general wants you to meet with him in his office. We need for you to draw a diagram of the cavern. He knows KY and his men had placed some explosives there but we believe the entrance has been reestablished", explained Wally.

Wally, Paul, and Wynnie entered the general's office. Since Paul, Wally, and Wynnie had left, a table had been set up in the general's office. A computer like device was on the table. The general entered from a door off of his office and instructed the man with him to "fire it up, Ken".

Ken sat down and a hologram image appeared in the middle of the table above a black gridded square.
"Kenny here will enter in your input on the cavern. We need to be able to send this information to all the troops in the field", replied the general.
"I entered through the main entrance. There were pockets of stalagmites to the right of the path. There were small areas behind the stalagmites that I was able to hide in", stated Paul.
"Where was the city" asked the general?
"I entered different areas by following the pathway downward. When they stopped at a wall, I pushed on the left side of the wall. It moved like a revolving door", explained Paul.
"How many levels did you manage to descent" asked the general?
"The city was on the third level down. The city was to the right of the path I was on. I continued downward two additional levels. That is when I found Wynnie. I helped her out of the cavern. I'm not sure if there were more levels beyond where Wynnie was being held or not", replied Paul.
"Wynnie, can you give me an idea of the layout of the level you were housed on" asked the general?

"There were rooms along the left side of the path for the woman they held captive. There was an underground lake of fresh water beyond the rooms on the left. As I continued to the right of the path, there were rooms being used as nurseries for the baby aliens and a delivery room for the captive pregnant women who were in active labor. I didn't get a chance to go through the door at the back of the nursery or delivery room. The aliens came in from there. I am sorry. I have very little knowledge of what is on the other side of the doorway", stated Wynnie.

Kenny's hand moved quickly on the computer keys. Soon the image of the cavern appeared above the black grid. Levels within the cavern slowly appeared as Kenny continued to stroke the computer keys.

"The entrance was more forward and the path started further inside the mouth of the cavern" stated Paul.

Kenny typed on the keys again and the image adjusted itself to the cavern Paul had just described.

"The city was a fair distance from the path. Maybe a couple football fields away", said Paul.

"What did the city look like" asked the general?

"Adobe like. The ceiling or area above was florescent. I could see windows in the buildings. I wasn't close enough to see pathways or residents" explained Paul.

"Rudy said the human germs were harmful to them so we humans had to be separated from them. It was odd because they kept the newborn aliens on the same level", stated Wynnie.

"Who is Rudy" asked the general?

"He is one of the evil aliens. He runs the human birthing area. I don't know where they grow or prepare the food they serve. It is like bean sprouts or bok choy. They supposedly supplement vitamins in the food. Their breakfast looks like green ground up oats", explained Wynnie.

"This must be their main location. We will need to use gas to stop them. Then we will need to eliminate the entire population", exclaimed the general.

"Ky and his team are on the front lines. The evil aliens have radioactive drones they bred to kill humans. I don't know what they look like up close but they move slowly and have a blue glow", said Wynnie.

The general picked up his phone and said, "Are the men ready with the hazmat suits? We will need lead shielding for our men slated in the area in and around the cave". The general listened intently to the person on the other end of the telephone then replied, "send the sergeant in to my office" and then hung up the telephone.

Soon another knock was heard on the general's door.

"Enter", yelled the general.

"I was told you wanted to see me, sir", stated the sergeant.

"Yes, I need weapons for these two civilians, including on person combat gear", stated the general. Wynnie and Paul looked at each other. Wynnie mouthed to Paul, "Combat gear?"

Paul shrugged his shoulders.

The sergeant left and the general spoke, "I know this is strange to you but this is new territory. We've never had to battle aliens' from another world. We can barely comprehend what weapons they may have or what fighting capabilities we may encounter".

The sergeant returned with a cart full of supplies. Wynnie and Paul was instructed to follow the sergeant to the room across the hall.

"My name is Bruce. The general wants you outfitted in combat gear. I can help you with your weapons once we have you in your weapons gear. You'll need camouflage fatigues". Wynnie choose to change in the bathroom and Paul said he'd change in the room he and Bruce were currently in. Bruce gave each a shirt, pants, socks and different colored boots. A cap and a jacket were given to Wynnie and Paul next.

"When you two are dressed, we'll go over your weapons", said Bruce.

Wynnie changed in the bathroom then knocked on the bathroom door. "Is it safe to come out?"

Bruce and Paul said, "Yes", in unison. Wynnie and Paul stood in front of Bruce's cart. Bruce spoke as he demonstrated. "This knife goes into the sheath on the left side of your belt. Your gun goes into the holster on the right".

"My what?" Asked Wynnie with a higher tone in her voice.

"Your gun. The general ordered you to be combat ready", stated Bruce.

"I've never held a gun. I don't know if I could shoot one", stated Wynnie.

"It's better to have one and not use it but carry it just in case", stated Bruce.

Wynnie looked distressed.

"Stick by me. Hopefully we won't have a need for any of the weapons", replied Paul.

Bruce continued, "Your hand grenades are on your left behind your knife".

Wynnie looked even more worried and asked, "Can any of this stuff go off by itself? I plan on staying hidden and out of the way."

"Are you certain you wouldn't rather stay here in the shelter until all this is over?" asked Paul.

"I'd feel trapped. Just like when I was stuck in the cavern", replied Wynnie.

Paul realized just how traumatized Wynnie must have been by the entire ordeal. "Just stay with Wally and me and we will all be fine", stated Paul.

Bruce helped Wynnie and Paul secure their utility belts. "Guess you are ready. Remember if you need to fire your weapon, aim at the chest if they are twenty feet away from you. Aim at the head if they are closer, instructed Bruce.

Wynnie took several deep breaths and said, "Ok, let's do this".

Wynnie and Paul knocked on the general's office door.

"Enter", commanded the general.

"What do you want us to do now"? Asked Wynnie.

"You will be escorted to our command center east of the cavern", replied the general. The general pushed a button on his desk. Soon Wally was at Wynnie's and Paul's side.

"These civilians are your responsibility. I want them safe but readily available in the event we have questions regarding our target. Now get going", instructed the general.

Wynnie, Paul, and Wally walked to the elevators.

"It seems odd having this secret bunker right in the middle of town. So many secrets", voiced Paul.

"Since you are officially in this battle, there are more interesting facts", stated Wally.

"Like what"? Asked Paul.

"Like space ships", stated Wally.

"Have you seen a space ship?" Asked Paul.

"I did get to see the outside of one", bragged Wally.

"Where?" Asked Paul.

"In one of the hangers in New Mexico", replied Wally.

"Boy, would I have loved to have been a fly on the wall. What a great story it would have been", stated Paul.

"All this information and this situation is confidential", exclaimed Wally.

"Yeah, that's the sad part of it. It would have been a really sensational story and I'm the guy who could have written it", said Paul.

Wally led Wynnie and Paul back to his jeep and said, "Climb in".

Wynnie sat in the back seat. Wally drove down back roads and through fields. Wynnie had no idea where they were. Wally stopped the jeep briefly, turned off the head lights, put on some odd looking goggles and began driving again. Wally drove safely wearing his funny goggles.

"What are those things Wally is wearing"? Asked Wynnie.

"Night goggles", replied Paul.

"I've heard of those. I didn't think they would actually work", replied Wynnie.

The ride ended in the middle of a forest area. There was a manufactured home hidden within the trees. Wally escorted Wynnie and Paul into the building. To left of the entrance door were eight monitor screens. A soldier sat in front of each screen and spoke into a head set device.

"Ok, these soldiers are monitoring a specific area. We need you to be readily available in the event an issue should arise that needs further information", stated Wally.

"Is there something we should be doing while we wait?" asked Paul.

"Just keep the coffee pot filled with strong, hot coffee for our guys in there. It looks like it will be a long night", stated Wally with a wink.

Wally led Wynnie and Paul onward and down a hallway. He entered a room to the right, off the hallway. There was a conference table with chairs surrounding the table. Wally continued onward through the room. A wall with a single door that was closed was on the far side of the room. Wally opened the door and continued to lead Wynnie and Paul into a wide open room. On one side of the room there was a sofa and soft recliner chairs. On the other side of the room was a kitchenette. A large pot of drip coffee was brewing.

"The refrigerator is stocked fresh every morning, noon, and early evening. There is fruit, yogurt, sandwiches, chicken wings, chicken fingers, salads, etc. In the freezer are pre-made meals. Help yourself when you get peckish", stated Wally.

Wally grabbed a cup and filled it with the warm fresh coffee. "I'll be in the other room with the other guys if you need me". He sipped on the hot beverage as he walked out of the room.

"So I guess we just sit here twiddling our thumbs until we are needed", said Wynnie.

"Basically, I guess so", replied Paul.

Wynnie walked over to the sofa, sat down and said, "Do you think they have any cards around this place?"

"Let's look", stated Paul as he began opening cabinet doors. Paul found the cards then walked over to Wynnie.

"What shall we play?" asked Wynnie.

"What card games do you know?" Asked Paul.

"Fish is about the only card game I know", Wynnie replied.

"Fish it is then", laughed Paul.

Paul and Wynnie played cards for hours. Unfortunately the card game did not distract their thoughts from where they were or why they were there. Paul stretched and said, "I think it's time for a break. How about a sandwich and a coke?"

"I think I'll stretch my legs a bit first. I hate being inside and all that jibber jabber from the other room is giving me a headache. I think I'll step outside and get a little air", replied Wynnie.

"Would you like me to come with you?" Asked Paul.

"Why don't you eat and then come out and join me", answered Wynnie.

"Don't you want something to eat?" asked Paul.

"I'll grab something a little later. Right now I need to move around a little. I feel like rigor mortis has set in", smiled Wynnie.

Just as Wynnie opened the door, Wally headed toward her.

"I thought I'd take a break and grab some grub", stated Wally.

"Great, you can join Paul. I'm just stepping outside for some air", replied Wynnie.

"Just stay close to the center. I don't know what type of animals maybe lurking about," instructed Wally.

"It's too dark to go out very far. I'll be nearby", replied Wynnie.

Wynnie stepped outside the command center. Once the door closed the sound of nature could be heard. A hoot owl could be heard in the distance. A cool breeze was a welcomed change from the stuffy room inside. Wynnie walked a few feet from the command center. Although the command center was surrounded by trees, there were areas of open ground. Wynnie walked to the area and looked up. The stars could be seen.

"Wow, do you look bright when there are no lights around", said Wynnie to the stars.

The sound of stirring in the bushes near the command center caught Wynnie's attention. Fear began to grow. Wynnie started walking back to the command center. Suddenly a rabbit hopped out of the foliage. Wynnie sighed in relief. "Oh my. I thought for sure you were going to harm me", she said to the rabbit. The rabbit suddenly scurried away.

"You don't have to be afraid of me", stated Wynnie to the rabbit.

"No, but he should be afraid of me", stated Stella as she emerged from the darkness of the trees several hundred feet away.

"Stella, you're safe. I'm so glad", replied Wynnie.

"Why would you be glad about that? You caused me to lose my home, my love, my purpose", confessed Stella.

"What are you talking about?" asked Wynnie.

"I was supposed to bear the child that would be the greatest leader of the new race. Then you came along and destroyed my dreams. You took everything away from me. Everything", yelled Stella as she walked toward Wynnie.

"Stella, you are just in shock. My friends can help you. Please let me get them", replied Wynnie as she slowly stepped in the direction of the command center.

"You aren't going to get anyone's attention except the attention of the mortician", exclaimed Stella. Stella lifted her right arm. Wynnie could see a gleam reflect off the blade of a very long knife that Stella was holding.

"It's time for you to die and believe me, this will bring me great pleasure", stated Stella as she quickened her pace toward Wynnie.

Suddenly a shot was heard. Stella stopped. She slowly lowered the knife. Stella was still staring at Wynnie as she dropped to her knees, then collapsed to the ground. Wynnie stood completely still. Wally and Paul raced out of the command center to find Wynnie in shock. Wynnie had somehow managed to grab her hand gun, point, and shoot Stella to protect herself.

Wally placed his hands over Wynnie's hand that held the gun. "You can let go now", Wally replied.

"She came out of the darkness. She had a knife. She was crazy. She said she wanted to kill me and ….." rattled Wynnie.

"You are alright. You had to defend yourself", stated Paul as he put his arm around Wynnie.

"It is odd seeing you upset when it was you that started this whole situation", stated Rudy as he stepped out of the darkness. Rudy had a bandage on his arm and was holding a weapon aimed at Wynnie.

Wally and Paul move in front of Wynnie.

"Gentlemen, do you really think you can keep me from taking what I came here for?" stated Rudy.

The door of the command center opened and four military personnel came out banishing weapons. One of Wally's men came around the back side of the command center and shoots his hand gun. The bullet hit Rudy in arm holding his gun. The gun drops to the ground.

"Come on, Pal. You have some talking to do", stated Wally to Rudy.

Wally had chains placed on Rudy's arms and legs.

"You will not hold me for long", stated Rudy.

"Well, my friend that is where you are very much mistaken. You see, General Wirwicz made certain to test myself and my men to make certain we couldn't be influenced by your mind games. You will be taken to one of our finest prison cells. I think there may be some questions we need to ask you", stated Wally as he escorted Rudy onto a truck.

The drive took almost two hours but soon, Rudy was locked into the prison cell Wally had mentioned. Rudy replied, "Do you think your human cage can hold me?"

"No, that is why I made one out of titanium", replied KY as he walked close to the cell door.

Shock could be seen on Rudy's face. Rudy stood and pushed on the bars of the cell. The bars held fast.

"Now I think is a good time for us to talk", stated KY.

"I will tell you nothing", exclaimed Rudy.

KY opened a small box. Two small devices hummed to life, zipped into the Rudy's cage and attached themselves to Rudy's neck.

"Your shock devices will not affect me", bragged Rudy.

"These have been modified", stated KY, "they screw a long thin wire into your brain. The electrical shock is not remembered but unfortunately, the process does destroy brain function. We end up getting the information we request".

Rudy realizes how futile it would be to resist. Rudy replies, "I do not wish to be harmed. I will tell you what you want to know".

Wynnie found herself back in the shelter, in bed, with the doctor caring for her. Paul was by her side.

"I'm glad you are feeling better", stated the doctor to Wynnie.

"Funny thing, I don't remember much of what happened", replied Wynnie.

"You went into shock, young lady", replied the doctor.

"I don't even remember my hand getting the gun out of the holster. I still have a hard time believing Stella was an alien sympathizer", said Wynnie.

"Well, you are safe and sound now", said the doctor, "and can be released from my care. Of course, I have to leave you in the hands of a responsible adult", stated the doctor.

"I'll take good care of her", replied Paul.

"What else happened out there?" asked Wynnie.

"Doctor, is it wise to tell her or should she just try and forget everything?" asked Paul.

"She needs to know", replied the doctor.

"After you saved yourself from Stella, Rudy came out of the woods for you", replied Paul.

"Why can't I remember that?" asked Wynnie.

"It was a sudden and frightening experience for you. Your brain protected you by blocking out the horrible experience", stated the doctor.

"After Rudy came out of the woods toward you with a gun in his hand. One of Wally's men flanked him and shot the weapon out of Rudy's hand. Wally and his men were able to capture Rudy and took him to prison. That should ease your mind", replied Paul.

"My mind won't be at ease until all this is over", stated Wynnie.

"Well, it's close to being over", stated Paul.

"What do you mean?" asked Wynnie.

KY and his two men, Lyk and Tyz, managed to place lethal gas in the alien city without getting captured", stated Paul.

"KY is ok?" Asked Wynnie.

"He sure is", replied Paul.

"What about the general and his troops?" Asked Wynnie.
"We are still working on that", stated General Wirwicz as he entered the room. "Sadly, soldiers follow what their commander orders. The soldiers may not recognize the general is an enemy of the people", continued General Wirwicz.
"Was the city destroyed?" Asked Wynnie.
"No, we are still setting the plan in motion on how to dispose of it", replied the general.
A knock at the door, followed by a soldier poking his head inside and saying, "We need you sir".
The general left the room. Moments later, Wally came in. "The general would like you both to accompany me to his office", said Wally.
"What's going on?" Asked Paul.
"KY and his team are securing the alien city. While in the cavern, KY came across the records of the alien births and their mothers. He has records of all the human women who were captured. The records are in alien script. KY and my team are translating them", stated Wally.
"They may be able to give some families some peace of mind on their loved ones that had gone missing", stated Paul.
Wynnic, Paul, and Wally walk to the general's office. Wally knocked on the general's door.
"Enter", said the general.
"I'm afraid I have some bad news", stated the general as he looked at Wynnie.
"You are looking at me as though I've grown an extra head. What is going on?" asked Wynnie.
"KY has been translating the records that were retrieved in the alien city. I'm afraid you were misled", stated the general to Wynnie.
"What do you mean, misled?" Asked Wynnie.
"According to KY, they decided you would be a perfect host to birth the children of the leader of the evil aliens", replied the general.

"Yes, well, they did steal my eggs", replied Wynnie.

"That is where you have been misled. You have been impregnated", stated the general.

Wally took Wynnie's arm and assisted her to a nearby chair. Paul looked just as stunned and confused as Wynnie.

"I can request the doctor eliminate this problem for you, if you want to rid yourself of this burden. It may help end the nightmare you have endured", offered the general.

"I'm afraid it isn't that easy general. Baby aliens will kill the mother if their needs are not met. I have no choice but to have this child, human or not", said Wynnie sadly.

"What can we offer you?" asked the general.

"I need to speak to KY", stated Wynnie.

The next morning, Wally escorted Wynnie to a conference room several corridors away from the general's office. KY and Paul was waiting for them.

"The records we retrieved indicate you were chosen by Rudy's superior as the vessel to grow his children. In an experiment, they have been attempting to blend human DNA with that of alien in hopes of creating a race that will not be affected by human pathogens. Alien fetus development is not in any way similar to that of human. We will need to care for you during the growth of the fetus to ensure its survival. We can also, find a family in which the child will be allowed to live, if it grows to full maturity", stated KY.

"Is Rudy's superior still alive?" asked Wynnie.

"No. My people have eliminated all the evil ones on this planet", stated KY."

"I need time to think", admits Wynnie.

"You have no time. We must supplement you with the needed enzymes for the fetus or the fetus will cause great harm to your body", stated KY.

"Are you really up to becoming a single mother?" asked Paul.

"I can't answer that question right now. I need time to sort all this out", exclaimed Wynnie.

"How long do I have to make a decision?" Wynnie asked KY.

"Maybe two days. The sooner we begin your supplements, the better it will be for the fetus and you", stated KY.

"I need some time alone", stated Wynnie. The general instructed Wally to find Wynnie a room in which she could rest and think. Wally led Wynnie down the hallway and to a small room. The room held a bed, a sofa and had a bathroom. No other luxuries could be seen. Wally hugged Wynnie and said, "Remember, you have us. You aren't alone".

Wynnie nodded her acknowledgement that she knew and understood.

Wynnie laid down on the bed. Thoughts clouded by questions kept racing through her mind.

What if the baby was born odd looking? What if the baby had health issues? Who would care for an alien baby? Will the baby be able to eat human foods? What kind of intelligence or abilities would the baby have?

Wynnie walked to the general's office and knocked.

"Enter", stated the general.

"I need to speak with KY again", exclaimed Wynnie.

The general dialed a number. "Get a hold of KY. Bring him to my office", stated the general to the person on the end of the phone line.

"Are you sure KY and his people were able to stop all the evil aliens?" asked Wynnie.

"Yes, and most of the children too", stated the general.

"What do you mean, most of the children too?" asked Wynnie.

"According to KY, alien children are very advanced. If they are guided the wrong way when they are young, then their intelligence tends to develop along that line. KY and his group felt the need to destroy most of the children", stated the general.

"How awful", replied Wynnie.

"War and the taking of lives is never a good thing. It is only done when absolutely necessary. In this case, we can see, it was absolutely necessary. Don't you agree?", replied the general.

"If their race is so smart, then how is it that the children can't be redirected toward the correct way?" asked Wynnie.

"I guess you will have to ask KY that question", replied the general.

"Will you let Paul know I'll call him when I get all of this sorted out? Right now, I have no choice but to have this child. I need to speak with KY", stated Wynnie.

KY entered the general's office. Wynnie didn't know how to say it, but she needed KY.

"Is your offer to help me through this pregnancy still available?" Asked Wynnie.

"Yes, I have already made all the arrangements for you and your child. With the general's permission, he can arrange for us to return to the area of my people", stated KY.

Wynnie found herself being escorted into a paneled van. The seating was comfortable but there were no windows in the van. A television was built into the ceiling and movies were available to be watched during the drive. Wynnie was being driven to an unknown location and she had no way to know the route to get in or out of what would soon be her new residence.

Hours later, the van stopped briefly, then resumed for about thirty minutes. When it stopped, Wynnie heard the engine stop too. She was where she needed to be, where ever that was. The door opened and a soldier guided Wynnie to a door. Through the door, KY met Wynnie.

"You will have your own room. My people will help you through this pregnancy. You will need supplements daily to ensure adequate survival of you and the fetus", stated KY.

"What do you mean when you say, me and the fetus?" asked Wynnie.

"If the fetus does not receive the enzymes needed for growth, the fetus will devour the mother to obtain those enzymes", informed KY.

"I don't know if I can handle this", announced Wynnie.

"You will only need to endure this for three months", replied KY.

"I still can't understand how your race manages to develop so quickly", stated Wynnie.

"It is the enzymes and the way our bodies metabolize them", stated KY.

"I want to learn everything I can about your race so I can ensure the health and well-being of this baby", stated Wynnie.

"This child will not be able to leave with you when you are able to go home", said KY.

"Oh, the germ thing. I hadn't thought about that", replied Wynnie.

"It is not only the micropathogens that are the problem. This fetus will develop differently from other children and therefore cannot be around humans", stated KY.

"I don't understand", said Wynnie.

"For the next three months, my people will educate you on our ways. You will understand when it is time for you to leave", replied KY.

"I can't leave my child. I may not have had a say in this pregnancy, but I'm definitely not leaving without my baby", stated Wynnie.

"We shall wait and see when you have been educated on my people and our ways. For now, let me show you your room", said KY as he began walking in the direction of an entrance to a strange looking hallway.

KY and Wynnie were met with soldiers guarding an elevator. The soldiers moved out of the way to allow KY and Wynnie to enter the large elevator. KY typed in a code and the elevator descended. Wynnie was nervous. She wished Paul could be with her. Until she discovered she was pregnant with an alien child, she had hoped her and Paul might develop a more permanent relationship.

When the elevator stopped and the doors opened, Paul was standing off to the side.

"Paul, you are here", screamed Wynnie excitedly as she wrapped her arms around his waist and hugged him firmly.

"KY asked me to come. He thought maybe you could use a human friend", said Paul with a smile.

"You both have proven yourselves to be friends of my people. You will be welcomed into our environment", stated KY.

"KY, I owe you an apology. I thought you were just like the evil aliens. I realize now I was very wrong to misjudge you. I hope you will accept my apologies", said Wynnie.

"Your fears were logical. You have a brave heart", replied KY.

Wynnie looked puzzled.

"What is the matter?" asked Paul.

"I don't understand what KY means when he says I have a brave heart", replied Wynnie.

"There is a legend that my people thought could never be fulfilled. You have rekindled our belief in that legend", stated KY.

"How could I have done that?" asked Wynnie.

"It is believed that from bad comes good. The legend was written eons ago. From good, evil will grow. Evil will find its way to a new world. Although evil will thrive it will eventually die. Good will come from evil. My people believe your fetus is our next queen", stated KY.

"My….. My child?" stuttered Wynnie as she held her abdomen.

"Your child came from evil. Evil has been destroyed. Your child will be raised with good intentions. Is that what you mean?" asked Paul.

"Simply stated, but yes", replied KY.

KY continued to escort Wynnie and Paul as he walked through a set of double doors. The environment changed. The ground was of soft dirt. Plants were abundant but they weren't like any plants Wynnie and Paul had ever seen before. The air became cooler and moist.

"The air smells earthy", replied Wynnie.

"Yes, my home planet is very indigenous. My people live simply and appreciate the purity of the air, water, and soil. We were intelligent enough to realize not to pollute our world", stated KY.

"I wish our people had been smarter. We had a stupid and greedy president who allowed our planet to be poisoned so he, his family, and his friends could make more money. Fortunately the American citizens came to their senses and booted them out of office", said Wynnie.

"Most humans can be fooled very easily", replied KY.

"Your race was fooled by Rudy and his group", replied Wynnie.

"It was not that we were fooled, but unaware. As we have all seen and can agree, evil and greed will try to take advantage of every race", stated KY.

A pleasant scent filled the air as KY, Wynnie, and Paul walked further into the foliage filled area.

"Is this a building or a cave?" asked Paul.

"It is both. Your government has agreed to house and protect us in exchange for our technology", stated KY.

"How can you have such advanced technology if you don't have motors or equipment and such?" asked Wynnie.

Much of our technology is developed in our minds. We share our thoughts with others when we wish too. We share our thoughts with others who specialize in technology. The schematics are worked out in our brains. If we all agree the idea can be useful, we build it. All of our laboratories for building any projects are located in one area. This serves several purposes. It contains any danger to one area. All the scientific brains are readily available and our environment will never be changed if there happens to be a problem", stated KY.

"What kind of technology do you have?" asked Wynnie.

"We have learned how to feed the energy cells in our bodies to prevent aging. In humans this cell is call the mitochondria", said KY.

"How long can your people live?" asked Wynnie?

"If I put our age in your language, centuries", replied KY.

"Centuries?" questioned Wynnie.

"A multitude of centuries", stated KY.

"When you first came to our planet, what year was it, in our time?" asked Paul.

"My people and I arrived before your pyramids were built", said KY.

"Amazing that you may know so much more about our history than we probably do", replied Wynnie.

"Some of my people arrived in the Antarctic region first. My son and I assisted to build a few of the pyramids. We placed a beacon there to signal our people", replied KY, "Rudy and my people have been battling since my people first arrived. Centuries later, more of my people arrived. One ship arrived in the Russian area. They knew the population was scarce so my people used nuclear means to stop the evils ones that were there. It was an air battle. The evil ones had their war ship ready when my people arrived. My people were fortunate enough to destroy the evil ones. It was a huge blast. As your world began to grow, my people placed a word here and there that spread. People began to believe it was a meteor that had struck the area. This helped us to remain hidden among humans".

"I had heard that meteor hit Russia in 1908", said Paul.

"It was June 30, 1908 to be exact, in Siberia. We shot down of their ships carrying iron. We were able to convince the earth people it was a meteor", stated KY.

"You said you came before the building of the pyramids?" asked Paul.

"Yes, my people showed them how to not only build the pyramids but how to put air and lighting inside them as well", replied KY.

"Why didn't you stay there?" asked Paul.

"The evils ones arrived. A battle ensued. We managed to chase them off but not before they destroyed what you know as the Sphinx", stated KY.

"Is that how the face was destroyed?" asked Wynnie.

"Partly. There was a rider that had been carved on the back of the Sphinx. The evil ones removed it using laser technology", replied KY.

"That seems like an odd thing to do", stated Wynnie.

"The rider was carved in the likeness of my former leader. My people tried to stop them and the face of the Sphinx was damaged. Fortunately, the evil ones left the area", stated KY.

"Where did they go?" asked Wynnie.

"Japan", replied KY.

"Japan?" asked Paul.

"The evil ones decided to build pyramids in Japan. They attempted to place beacons on the pyramids to signal their groups who were still out in space. We discovered them before they could carve a fourth monument", stated KY.

"What did you do?" asked Paul.

"We caused a tsunami so large, the land with the pyramids ended up underwater. That would have been ten of your centuries ago", stated KY.

"How did the evil aliens get away?" asked Paul.

"They had sent out a small group to go ahead to see if they could find an area safe for them", stated KY.

"Where did that group end up at?" asked Wynnie.

"South America. Guatemala. They managed to build multiple pyramids", replied KY.

"Why pyramids?" asked Paul.

"They stood high enough to place a signal beacon on. They stood well above local landscape and could be easily spotted from space", replied KY.

"You managed to find them again?" asked Paul.

"No, the heat, humidity, and human bred micropathogens caused them move before we could find them", stated KY.

"Then how did both your groups end up on the same continent?" asked Paul.

"My people decided to go where there had been no pyramids built. We came to what you now call the United States", replied KY.

"How long had it been before you discovered Rudy and his people were here?" asked Paul.

"We had built several pyramids on the southern portion of the peninsula you call Florida. I had gone back to check on the others position in the middle east, Guatemala, Japan, and, Russia. While I was gone, another group of Rudy's arrived. Rudy convinced this new group to attack my people. They created a hurricane by which none of earths people have ever seen before or ever again. It caused the ocean bottom to sink, taking with it our pyramids. My son was able to destroy the new group of evil aliens. Rudy and a few of his men escaped. My son waited for me to return", replied KY.

"Could your son have ended this if he had followed Rudy?" asked Paul.

"Yes", replied KY.

"Then why did he wait?" asked Wynnie.

"Because his mother was injured in the battle. He stayed with her. She died several of your days later. My son was understandably upset", stated KY.

"I'm sorry. I didn't realize", stated Wynnie.

"I was angry too. I told my son his mother had died unnecessarily. He had allowed her killers to go free", stated KY.

"What did he say?" asked Wynnie.

"He didn't say anything. He left during the night. He left a message saying he would find me when he found the evil ones", stated KY.

"Didn't you say your son was killed over Roswell?" asked Wynnie.

"Yes. Rudy and his people had started watching the skies for my people. My son was not as experienced as he could have been when it came to war maneuvers. As I mentioned before, my race is a peaceful one. I had centuries of practice and learning to fight the evil ones. My son had very little experience. He flew right into a trap they had set", stated KY.

"How awful", replied Wynnie.

"What kind of a trap"? Asked Paul

"They had sent up space flares. To my son, he must have believed it was the evil ones space craft. When he flew towards the flares, they shot his ship down. I understand he was alive when the humans found him", exclaimed KY.

"What"? Questioned Paul.

"Yes, he was still alive. His three other crew members were killed on impact", reported KY.

"What happened to him"? Asked Paul.

"That story will have to wait for another time. We are here", stated KY.

"Here"? Asked Wynnie and Paul in unison.

"Your rooms", replied KY.

"Our rooms"? Questioned Paul.

"Yes. I believed I mentioned it may be helpful if Wynnie had a human friend with her during this time of growth", stated KY.

"Yes, but you didn't say I'd have to stay here", replied Paul.

"This area is highly classified. The less activity on the outside the better or so I have been told. Therefore, when I spoke of Wynnie's need for human interaction, General Wirwicz suggested I contact you. I thought you understood the need for secrecy", replied KY.

"Yes, but that doesn't mean I shouldn't be allowed to go home at night", replied Paul.

"I didn't realize I would have to stay either. Why can't I get a bottle of your special enzymes to take and stay on the base"? Asked Wynnie.

"It would look very queer for your pregnancy to develop so quickly", said KY.

"I didn't think of that", replied Wynnie.

"That does make sense, for Wynnie to stay but it doesn't explain why I have to stay", stated Paul.

"Paul is right. He shouldn't be stuck here just because of my situation", stated Wynnie.

"The general and I spoke in great lengths about the situation. We believe we can make you both feel better regarding this situation. My people and I will allow you both access to our library", stated KY.

Paul and Wynnie's facial expressions showed shock.

"We have an audio translator that will allow you to discover the history of my people, our technologies, our culture, values, and other facts. The general mentioned that Paul may find a story he could write. The general did mention the words, undisclosed source", stated KY.

"I would like to learn about your people. Not just because of my baby will be part alien, but because I consider you a friend", announced Wynnie.

"So it is agreed", stated KY.

Paul and Wynnie looked back from the direction in which they had recently walked. They could not see the entrance.

"Your rooms are in the same area. Wynnie's room is here. Paul, your room is around the corner. Food will be brought into you daily. Eat as much and as often as you desire. Tomorrow I will show you around the village", said KY.

"I am confused. Rudy and his people had to be away from humans because of our germs. Would our germs affect you too"? Asked Wynnie.

"Tomorrow it will all be explained. Please, orient yourselves to your new rooms. I will escort you around tomorrow", stated KY.

Paul and Wynnie agreed and they walked into the first of their assigned rooms. Wally was sitting on a chair in the first room Wynnie and Paul walked into.

"What are you doing here"? Asked Paul.

"That is the thanks I get for hooking you up to the biggest story of your life", stated Wally.

"I don't get it. What are you talking about"? Asked Paul.

"I explained to the general how this entire ordeal has cost you multiple stories. The general felt the government owed you and decided to help you find your next story. Of course, you can't write about the aliens, but you can write about one of a hundred technological devices they have. Did you know they have a machine that controls the weather? They use low frequency radio waves and it somehow works. They have a laser that can cut into solid stone and a device that can displace the stone's atoms? That is how they built this mountain village", stated Wally.

"You're kidding me, aren't you"? Asked Paul.

"Nope. You'll see. By the way, you look beautiful Wynnie. Motherhood becomes you", said Wally as he rose and kissed her on the cheek.

"Thank you Wally. I think you are exaggerating. I am exhausted all the time", replied Wynnie.

"You won't' be for long. KY has supplements to make you energized. I guess he'll talk to you about all that stuff soon. So did you see your rooms yet"? Asked Wally.

"No, we just arrived", stated Paul.

"Paul, you'll love the shower. Water drenches you from almost every angle. Nice hot water. They make some kind of chemical free soap that makes your skin as soft as a baby's bottom", bragged Wally.

"I can't wait to try that", stated Paul.

"Wynnie, you will love the foot bath. You can soak your feet while resting in one of their mobile chairs. I use to think I had a great recliner until I tried those. You almost never want to get out of the water", smiled Wally.

It seems only minutes had passed when two alien women entered pushing a cart full of food. They said nothing but left the cart slightly inside the entrance to Wynnie's room.

"Just in time", stated Wally, "I'm starving".

The cart was filled with various colored foods. The food was oddly different. Small pancakes filled one bowl. Triangle shaped greens filled another bowl. Wally poured three glasses of florescent purple beverage. Paul and Wynnie looked at the liquid.

"It tastes better than it looks", stated Wally. Paul took a sip. "It's good", replied Paul. Wynnie tasted it.

"Yum, it tastes like bananas and strawberries", she replied. Then Wally picked up what looked like an orange egg roll.

"These are delicious. It is all organic. These taste like oranges but it is some kind of protein. Those green triangles taste like fritters", stated Wally.

"Well, this will be an adventure", stated Paul.

Wally began filling everyone's plates with various items. Wynnie hesitated with each new item but found herself enjoying everything she tried. Wally, Wynnie, and Paul ate until they were all about to burst.

"I am stuffed", stated Paul.

The group moved to the sitting area.

Paul noticed Wynnie looked sad. "Are you ok"? He asked.

"I'm nervous. I still have no idea what to say to my folks. I don't know what I will do financially either. I was helping my parents with the bills. This entire situation has put me and them in a spot and it's all my fault. Not only that, but I thought there would be humans here. I didn't realize I'd be locked away", said Wynnie with tears in her eyes.

Wally put his arm around Wynnie and said, "The general told me he is prepared to take responsibility for your situation. He believed he owes you some form of compensation. If general McMurrer had been true to his country, you would not have been placed in this situation. With that said, General Wirwicz would like to financially compensate you for the time you will be having this extended stay. He told me to convey that to you", stated Wally."

"That will help with my financial situation, but I still have no idea what to say to my folks", stated Wynnie.

"How about an educational leave. The general said he could offer you advanced educational materials. You can tell your folks you signed up for a local educational course. You can even say it's like an internship. You earn while you learn", stated Wally.

"I'm not really good at cover stories. My parents would know I wasn't telling the truth", stated Wynnie.

"But you will be telling the truth. You will be learning about aliens. Your parents don't need to know they aren't aliens from another country. Just leave that part out", suggested Wally.

Wally arranged for a laptop computer to be used. He escorted Wynnie to the computer area.

"This is the only area that is set up to get Wi-Fi", stated Wally.

Wynnie skyped with her folks.

"How long will you be gone"? Asked Mom.

"It depends on the courses and how well everyone does", replied Wynnie.

"Will you be coming home at all before you do these classes"? Asked dad.

"I won't have time. I am sorry this is such short notice. It's something that I can't walk away from", admitted Wynnie.

"Well, write often and let us know how you are doing. Maybe dad and me can't break away and come see you", stated Mom.

"That isn't possible. They have strict rules for who is allowed in the area", stated Wynnie.

"Then you better promise to keep in touch either by letter or phone", insisted Mom.

"I promise", said Wynnie, "I'd better go. I don't want to be late".

The screen went black as Wally ended the call.

Suddenly Wynnie doubled over with pain. Wally raced to get help. Paul stayed at Wynnie's side.

An alien woman arrived. She stood over Wynnie and closed her eyes. As suddenly as the pain had started, it stopped.

"How did you do that"? Asked Wynnie.

"I spoke to your daughter. You caused her distress. You must try to adapt and stop becoming so emotional", stated the alien woman and turned to leave.

"I'm having a girl. How can they know"? Asked Wynnie.

"They are really smart", replied Wally.

"I think I'll go lie down", said Wynnie.

"Would you like me to stay with you"? Asked Paul.

"You are right next door if I need anything. Right now I feel drained", replied Wynnie.

"If I don't hear from you before then, I will swing by tomorrow", announced Paul.

"Thank you both. I'm sorry if I've been moody", said Wynnie.

"I believe that comes with the territory", replied Wally as he walked over and kissed Wynnie on the cheek, then left.

"You sure you want to be alone"? Asked Paul.

"I'm not alone", said Wynnie with a sad smile. Paul left and Wynnie went to the bedroom. She laid on the bed. "Oh mom. I wish you were here", she said a tear streamed down her face. Wynnie managed to fall asleep. She awoke with a female alien standing near her bed.

"You need to take your enzymes now", instructed the alien woman.

Wynnie took the capsules and swallowed them with a glass of water. Surprisingly, Wynnie felt more energetic and happy only moments after swallowing the capsules. The alien woman left and KY entered.

"I will explain your regime", stated KY.

"I have a regime"? Asked Wynnie.

"For your welfare and that of your daughter", stated KY.

"How do you know I am having a daughter"? Asked Wynnie.

"I have spoken to her", replied KY.

"Excuse me"? Replied Wynnie.

"Humans are centuries behind my people. As I've mentioned before, we can read minds. My people communicate with our minds", replied KY.

"I'm stunned", replied Wynnie.

"I have prepared a list of the times your enzymes will be brought to you. Every two hours during what you call your waking hours. Every four hours during your sleep rotation", replied KY.

"Is this supplement really necessary so often"? Asked Wynnie.

"For the health of the fetus, yes", stated KY.

"Is there anything else I need to know"? Asked Wynnie.

"We need to apply a small device to your abdomen. It relays information to the fetus", replied KY.

"Apply how and what information"? Asked Wynnie.

"It is applied with an adhesive. It will be removed in less than three months. It is to give the fetus information as she grows", explained KY.

"Why less than three months"? Asked Wynnie.

"When the child is born", replied KY.

"I'd forgotten about the accelerated growth of alien babies", said Wynnie.

"We encourage you to eat our food. It will help the fetus grow healthier than if you consume human food", stated KY.

"Supplements and food. Anything else I should know"? Asked Wynnie.

"The fetus will tell us if she needs anything else", stated KY.

Wynnie had nothing to say to KY's last statement.

Wynnie followed KY's planned regime. She ate three meals a day, all alien food. Beverages were the ones that came with her meals or water. Wynnie wished she could have a nice tall glass of iced tea but didn't want to break the regime for the baby.

Wynnie's abdomen grew quickly. KY gave Wynnie a container of orange oil to apply to her abdomen daily before bed. The oil would help Wynnie's skin to endure the rapid stretching required for her baby's growth.

Wynnie lost count of the days. She, Paul and Wally spent a lot of time in the library. Using the auto-translator, Wynnie was able to read books about alien life. Paul researched alien technology with Wally.

Then one morning, KY came to visit Wynnie.

"Join me for breakfast"? Asked Wynnie.

"No. I will escort you to the birthing room. You will begin labor within two hours", stated KY.

"I bet human women wished they could predict when they'd go into labor. It will certainly stop a lot of babies from being born in cabs", replied Wynnie.

"I do not understand that statement", replied KY.

"It is unimportant", said Wynnie as she followed KY.

Haley was born the natural way. Although she was part alien she came into the world the human way, with a vaginal delivery. Wynnie only got a glimpse of her beautiful baby girl before a tall beautiful alien woman swept the infant away.

Labor had been surprisingly quick for this being Wynnie's first pregnancy. Wynnie was still quite fatigued. The military doctor had stayed with Wynnie after she had given birth. The doctor gave Wynnie a small dose of pain medication to allow Wynnie to rest.

Wynnie woke up several hours later. Paul and Wally were sitting nearby playing cards.

"Hey, our girl is awake", stated Wally.

"How are you feeling"? Asked Paul.

"Surprisingly well. Do you know when they will bring Hayley back to me"? Asked Wynnie.

"I believe the babies are cared for by specific care givers", stated Wally.

"I should be able to care for my own child", said Wynnie.

KY came into the room and said, "You are probably wanting to hold your baby".

"Yes, I am", replied Wynnie.

"For her safety, she is in our nursery", replied KY.

"What do you mean, for her safety"? Asked Wynnie.

"You must stop thinking of your baby as a normal baby. Her metabolism needs are very great at this time. We need to supplement her needs with appropriate enzymes, proteins, and vitamins", stated KY.

"Then when can I see her"? Asked Wynnie.

"In a day or two. When we have her more stabilized", replied KY.

Wynnie seemed sad.

"Can Wynnie go and see Hayley"? Asked Paul.

"It is better for the babies to be alone during the transition from their internal world to the external world. You will also need to recover from your pregnancy", stated KY.

"Humans believe in bonding. Mothers and babies are kept together", stated Wynnie.

"Your baby is only part human. She may look human but she is more like my people than yours. You will see her soon. Remember we want what is best for everyone", stated KY.

Paul went to Wynnie and said, "You do want what is best for your baby".

"KY, I'm not trying to argue with you. I just thought I'd be able to hold my baby, nurse her, and look at her. All this is new to me and to be separated from my new born child seems abnormal", explained Wynnie.

"In a few days, you will see your child. Rest and recuperate. All will be well", KY said as he walked to the door and left.

"Looks like I don't have a choice", replied Wynnie.

"You'll see her soon enough. Take advantage of the time to rest", suggested Wally.

A knock at the door and a beautiful alien woman entered and stated, "We need to pump your milk for your baby".

"That is our que to leave", replied Wally.

"We'll come back tomorrow. Is there anything we can bring you"? Asked Paul.

I'd like to write my parents. Would you be able to bring me some stationary, stamps, and a pen"? Asked Wynnie.

"Sure thing", replied Paul as he kissed Wynnie lightly on the lips.

Wynnie gave a tired grin and replied, "Thanks".

Two days later, Wynnie was sitting in her room when one of the tall beautiful women came in. In her arms was a baby that looked six months old.

"My baby is only two days old", replied Wynnie.

"Yes. This is she", replied the woman.

"How is that possible"? Asked Wynnie.

"Very high metabolism", replied the woman as she placed the baby in Wynnie's arms.

"She is such a beautiful baby", exclaimed Wynnie.

"Mama", replied Hayley.

"You can speak"? Asked Wynnie.

Hayley nodded yes.

"You understand me"? Asked Wynnie.

Hayley again nodded yes.

"Your child is very advanced compared to human babies. She can understand you and speak. She can stay with you for thirty minutes, then she will need to return to her pod", stated the alien woman.

"Her pod"? Questioned Wynnie.

"KY can explain our ways to you. I will return in twenty five minutes", said the woman.

Wynnie sat Hayley on her lap facing her. "You have your grandmother's eyes", said Wynnie.

"Blue", replied Hayley.

"Yes", smiled Wynnie, "Blue eyes. You are so beautiful".

"All babies are beautiful to their mothers", replied Hayley.

"It is so difficult to believe you have grown so quickly and can do so much", stated Wynnie.

Hayley just smiled at Wynnie.

Wynnie kissed Haley on her forehead. Hayley had a puzzled look on her face.

"I love you", stated Wynnie.

Hayley looked more puzzled.

"I will explain everything to you when you are older", said Wynnie.

Hayley laughed.

"Wow, you already have two teeth. Even your hair is long. Long and golden", stated Wynnie.

The woman came back and said, "Your child need her nutrition. The woman plucked Hayley from Wynnie's arms and quickly left.

"When can I see her again"? Called Wynnie loudly but the woman had gone.

Paul knocked and asked, "Can I come in"?

"Yes", replied Wynnie sadly.

"Are you ok"? Asked Paul.

"I was able to see Hayley for only twenty five minutes. She looked as if she were six months old. I have no idea when I'll be able to see her again. I feel as though I am a prisoner and my daughter is being kept away from me", stated Wynnie.

"You aren't a prisoner. If you get dressed, we can go for a walk", stated Paul.

"That is a good idea. I have been feeling a bit cabin crazy", replied Wynnie. Wynnie dressed quickly. She slid her feet into her shoes and joined Paul in the living area. Paul and Wynnie walked down the long hallway where most of the non-military personnel had rooms.

"Why don't we see if we can explore and who knows, maybe find ourselves a new adventure", stated Paul.

Wynnie smiled, "I do need a distraction".

Wynnie and Paul slowly walked down the hallway. When they came to another hallway, they stopped.

"Shall we go left or right"? Asked Paul.

"Left", replied Wynnie.

They walked slowly, looking in each room they came to. After they walked for nearly a thousand feet, they noticed a small corridor to the right. Paul looked at Wynnie and said, "Shall we"?

Wynnie nodded yes and Paul led the way. They had only walked several feet into the room when Paul opened a door to a very strange looking room. The room was huge. Inside the room were pod-like devices. In each pod, was an alien getting a rejuvenation and purification process.

"Come in", stated KY.

"What is all this"? Asked Paul.

"These pods are filters. They allow our people to be cleansed of the microorganism that can cause us illness or death", explained KY.

"So Ruddy was correct. Human germs can cause you harm", replied Wynnie.

"Yes, but your atmosphere can cause our bodies to experience changes. It is most difficult to explain the changes that occur. We must undergo this filtration process once weekly to remain healthy", stated KY.

"It looks like the person inside has oxygen on. Are they receiving oxygen or a gas of some type"? Asked Paul.

"Actually, it is oxygen. The pod is filled with filtration fluid", explained KY.

"That is amazing", replied Paul.

"It is almost like a womb", stated Wynnie.

"You would be a candidate for the pod", exclaimed KY.

"Me"? Asked Wynnie.

"Yes. You have had alien organisms within. The filtration fluid could cleanse you of any potential issues", suggested KY.

"What kind of issues"? Asked Paul.

"This is new territory. We don't know long term how Wynnie's body will react to the chemicals Rudy and his group introduced. We can prevent any future problems that we may need to face in the future", stated KY.

"Do you know something I haven't been informed of"? Asked Wynnie.

"No. We simply don't know what experiments Rudy and his people were performing on humans. I was merely offering you future peace of mind", stated KY.

"It seems so extreme", stated Wynnie.

"It is safe. It is a purification process", replied KY.

"Maybe you could explain more", said Paul.

"I cannot discuss the specifics. I can say, the pod cleanses and filters. You are safe and will feel incredible when the process is complete", stated KY.

"I can monitor things on the outside while you are on the inside", stated Paul.

"That is not allowed. The occupant is naked. No interruptions must occur during the filtration process", stated KY.

"How long does the process take"? Asked Paul.

"The duration varies depending on the status of the occupant", stated KY.

"I think you should try it. We don't know how screwy Rudy was and what he may have introduced into your body", stated Paul.

"I wish this nightmare would end", stated Wynnie.

"The pod may help in the recovery process", stated KY.

"What about Hayley. She was inside me. Wouldn't she have been introduced into whatever my body had been introduced to"? Asked Wynnie.

"Hayley has been purified", stated KY.

"But she's a child", stated Wynnie.

"As I explained, we need purified weekly. Because your daughter has been introduced to human germs for a greater length of time, she was given purification immediately after birth", stated KY.

"Ok. I'll do it too", replied Wynnie.

"You'll need to disrobe in the room to your right. I will have one of my female technicians assist you so you feel more comfortable", said KY.

"I'll wait for you in your room", said Paul.

Wynnie nodded her acknowledgement as she turned and entered the room to the right.

The room had a chair, shelves, a clothes rack with hooks. Wynnie had just sat down when a beautiful blonde woman came into the room.

"You'll need to remover everything", stated the woman.

"I recently gave birth", explained Wynnie.

"All feminine products must be removed as well before entering the pod. I have a robe for you to wear. I was informed you are too embarrassed about your body to walk to the pod", stated the woman.

"I'm not embarrassed, I am modest. There is a difference", explained Wynnie.

"You may wear your panties to the pod if it makes you feel less modest. However; everything must be removed before entering the pod", instructed the woman.

"Thanks. I think I'd prefer that", replied Wynnie.

The woman stood and waited for Wynnie to finish undressing.

"You are going to watch me undress"? Asked Wynnie.

"I am assisting you, not watching you. I need to ensure you are free of any items that may interfere with your purification process", stated the woman.

Wynnie began to undress.

"You will need to remove your earrings", stated the woman.

"Really"? Asked Wynnie.

"Yes, really", replied the woman.

Wynnie donned the robe then removed her earrings. She hung her clothing up, placed the earrings inside her shoe. She placed her socks inside her shoes and then placed her shoes on one of the empty shelves.

"I guess I am as ready as I'll ever be", replied Wynnie.

"You will need to remove your hair accessory", stated the woman.

Wynnie was a little annoyed but complied. She removed her hair clip and placed it inside one of her shoes.

"Follow me", instructed the woman.

Wynnie followed the woman into the pod room. Each pod was situated in a stall. The woman led Wynnie to the far end of the room.

"I have chosen this secluded pod in efforts to assist you to feel more comfortable", stated the woman.

Wynnie felt badly for misjudging the woman. "I do appreciate that", replied Wynnie.

"You can keep your robe on until it is time to enter the pod", said the woman.

"Isn't it time now"? Asked Wynnie.

"No. First I will get you ready", stated the woman.

"How do you get me ready"? Asked Wynnie.

The woman reached behind the pod to a small shelf and removed long tubes. "This tube is like the scuba gear your under water divers use. Of course, they are made of special material that will not interfere with your purification process", stated the woman.

The woman reached to a small cabinet behind the pod. When the woman opened her hand, Wynnie saw an odd looking device.

"What does that do"? Asked Wynnie.

"In simple terms, it plugs your nose", stated the woman.

The woman showed Wynnie how to insert the small cushioned device in her nose. There was a small clear strip on each of the cushioned device.

"Place this mouth piece in your mouth. It is designed so the first portion goes behind your teeth while the second portion secures in front of you teeth. When you bite down, the device will mold to your mouth and form a nice seal. The tubing attaches in the front", said the woman.

Wynnie could feel cool moist air flowing into her mouth.

"Breath in and out through your mouth. Remember, your nose is plugged", said the woman as she attached a clip with an elastic band to one side of the cushioned nose plug. The woman then stretched and secured the elastic band to the other side of the nose plug. Wynnie could feel the nose plug was secured in place.

"You will need to remove your panties and robe before entering into the pod. There is an area inside the pod in which you can lie comfortably", instructed the woman.

Wynnie removed the rest of her garb and climbed into the pod.

"Please lie down", instructed the woman.

Wynnie sat on the make shift lounger. The woman spoke as she closed and latched the pod door.

"Breath slowly. The pod will begin to fill with purification fluid. You are completely safe", spoke the woman as she turned some small knob near the tubing.

Wynnie closed her eyes and thought, "I'm naked and scuba diving in an alien tank. I hardly feel safe".

Suddenly the cool moist air had the taste of citrus. Wynnie felt herself getting increasingly sleepy. She could hear the sound of water. It almost sounded like waves lapping at the shore. Music began to play softly. Wynnie drifted off into slumber.

The pod filled completely with the purifying fluid. The warm liquid engulfed Wynnie and her body floated effortlessly in the pod.

When Wynnie awoke, she was dressed in a silk night gown. She had no idea how she had gotten dressed or how she had gotten in the bed she now occupied. She felt amazingly good.

"Your body has mended and is now perfectly healthy", stated KY.

"What do you mean, mended? Was there damage from the alien chemicals"? Asked Wynnie.

"No, but your body has returned to its pre-pregnant state", replied KY.

"How is that possible"? Asked Wynnie.

"I cannot explain how it works. It filtrates and purifies. It promotes healing", replied KY.

"My skin feels so soft", stated Wynnie as she stroked her arm.

"You may return to your room now. The process is complete", stated KY.

There were slippers ready and waiting for Wynnie. She slid her feet into the slippers and stood. Wynnie felt her abdomen. It felt flat and firm. Wynnie felt fantastic. She followed KY as he guided her through the maze of hallways back to her room.

"You will see your daughter tomorrow", stated KY.

Wynnie grinned as she entered her room. Paul was asleep on her bed.

"Hello, sleepy head", called Wynnie loudly.

Paul opened his eyes. "Wow. I must have dozed off", he said.

"You think", said Wynnie with a giggle.

"You look beautiful. Now I know why it took you so long. You had the spa treatment", stated Paul.

"What do you mean"? Asked Wynnie.

"You had your hair done", replied Paul.

Wynnie had not realized her hair which normally curled and rested on her shoulders had been braided. She walked to the bathroom to view herself in the mirror and gasped at the sight she saw. Her hair was no longer the shiny brunette color but was now pale yellow.

"I didn't dye my hair", stated Wynnie to Paul, "I need to speak to KY and find out why they did this to me".

When Paul finally got Wynnie to calm down, he went to find KY.

KY entered Wynnie's room and stated, "I was told you were upset with your rejuvenation".

"Rejuvenation. You call this rejuvenation"? Stated Wynnie holding up her hair.

"You must have alien genetic coding in your system. Maybe it was the exchange of blood from mother to fetus that may have mapped your cells. Our pods repair the participant to their optimal state. Your body is now as it once was before your pregnancy. Any microorganism or pathogens have been completely removed", stated KY.

"If that is true, then how did this happen"? Asked Wynnie.

"As I have stated, I cannot share the mechanisms with you", said KY.

"I mean, why would my hair change colors"? Asked Wynnie.

"Because alien genetics are superior to human. Your cells have taken on the better improvement between the two", replied KY.

"You didn't say anything about my hair being changed. You said it would protect me from alien germs", replied Wynnie.

"What is done cannot be undone. Is there anything else"? Asked KY.

"Yes. I want to leave and I want my daughter", exclaimed Wynnie.

"That is not possible. Your child would die within hours if she were to leave our care", stated KY.

"KY, could you give Wynnie and me some privacy? I need to talk to her", stated Paul.

"I shall be nearby in the event I am needed", stated KY as he turned to leave.

"Wynnie, I know you've been through a lot. You have gotten the raw end of the deal at every turn. No one is denying you haven't been dealing with a lot of changes that pushed you into a corner. But I know you wouldn't do anything that would hurt Hayley", stated Paul.

"I have no control. None! I can only see my daughter when they allow me to. I can't leave this place until I've been officially debriefed. They won't hold my debriefing sessions for another three weeks. I am going crazy", stated Wynnie, "and now my hair".

One of the female aliens entered Wynnie's room. "Excuse me. KY sent me. He instructed me to give you access to our ancient files".

Wynnie looked at Paul. "What is in your ancient files that would pertain to me"? Asked Wynnie.

"I am certain I do not know. KY believes you may feel differently if you knew the heritage and growth process of your daughter", replied the woman.

"Sounds like a good idea. It may keep your mind off your troubles", replied Paul.

"Only if you come with me", stated Wynnie.

"You bet", replied Paul.

Wynnie and Paul followed the alien woman through a labyrinth of hallways that seemed to have no reasonable sense to the layout. Finally the woman stopped at an odd looking entrance way.

"There is a small area you must pass through. You must go one at a time. There is a one minute delay between entries. A scanner will scan you then you will be admitted to the ancient file room", instructed the woman.

"Shall I go first"? Asked Paul. Wynnie nodded yes.

"See you on the other side", stated Paul as he opened the door and entered. The woman closed the door after Paul had entered. The woman waited with Wynnie. An odd noise was heard, then a bright light escaped around the door's edges. When the light was gone, the odd noise was heard again. The woman opened the door and instructed Wynnie to enter.

Wynnie slowly entered. The entrance was like a small closet. The woman closed the door behind Wynnie. A strange noise could be heard. Suddenly, a very bright light scanned Wynnie from head to toe. Wynnie closed her eyes. The light was painful to her eyes. When Wynnie hear the odd noise again, she opened her eyes. A door opened in the opposite direction of where Wynnie had entered. Paul was waiting for her as she walked out of the entrance into the adjacent room.

The room was bright but no visible light source could be seen. A device was in the middle of the room. Wynnie and Paul went to examine the device. It had a very thin opening that looked like a giant coin slot. Shelves were attached to the device. Small clear coins were stacked side by side on the shelves. Paul said, "I think I know what this is", as he removed on of the clear coins and inserted it into the slot on the device.

The device began to slowly descend into an area below the floor. A cushioned seat ascended from the floor near the back of the room. The room began to darken. Paul took Wynnie's hand and led her to the cushioned seat. "Let's see what movie is showing", he said with a smile.

An image appeared. A woman in labor with helpful family members nearby. It actually looked as though a woman was giving birth in the middle of the room. How the device was able to project such a life like image had Wynnie and Paul amazed. The next image was of the baby in the arms of the mother. The baby was being given a dark yellow liquid and what appeared to be strips of meat.

The infant was placed in a round cushion. The baby was fed every two hours. A time appeared prior to each and every scene. The infant grew amazingly quick. The time span increased in speed. The young alien grew at an alarming rate. Within days the child appeared to be 7 years old. The child spent only an hour or two with the child's mother. The child spent the remainder of the day in a room filled with what looked like monitor screens with a variety of educational programs running simultaneously. How the child could absorb any information at all with all the distraction of noise and pictures was a mystery.

When the child was what Wynnie calculated to be six days old, the child had grown to adulthood. The infant was less than a week of age and yet was fully grown. The mother of the child rested for days. Food and drink was catered to the mother.

When the mother was strong enough, she was assisted to a pod identical to the pod Wynnie had been placed in. The mother looked fatigued and her abdomen had the post-delivery bulge. The woman disrobed and stepped into the pod. The equipment to breath was applied. The pod door was sealed and the woman rested in the built in chair as the fluid slowly engulfed her body.

Time elapsed quickly. Eight hours had gone by. The pod fluid slowly drained. Several alien women assisted the still sleeping occupant onto a gurney-like stretcher. The alien women took the mother to a shower room. The mother remained asleep as the two alien woman rinsed her hair and body of the purification fluid. They braided the mother's hair, oiled her skin and dressed her.

The mother woke up hours later in her own bed. Her tummy bulge was gone and she looked years younger. When the women's daughter returned, the two looked like sisters. The mother and daughter began speaking in their native language. It was at that point that the scene ended and the machine with the shelves full of clear disc returned.

"I'm not sure why KY wanted me to have access to this room", replied Wynnie.

"There are more disc to watch. Maybe we chose the wrong one", replied Paul.

Wynnie walked over to the shelves and picked up a clear disc from the middle of the top shelf. She inserted the disc into the coin like slot and the machine again descended below the floor.

Wynnie walked back and sat near Paul. The room began to darken. The scene began with a handsome alien man came into view. He was speaking in his alien dialect to a group of other aliens. You could see the group agreed with whatever it was the handsome alien man had said.

"He must be their leader", stated Wynnie.

Soon the handsome leader was seen walking through a dark hallway. The hallway seemed familiar somehow. Paul must have had the same feeling because he sat up straighter and leaned forward.

When the handsome alien moved a stone wall, a woman could be seen lying on a table. Her hands were tied at her side and her feet elevated and tied. The handsome alien walked closer. Wynnie gasped. The handsome alien was looking her.

"You don't need to watch this", exclaimed Paul.

"Yes, I do", replied Wynnie.

The handsome alien removed his clothes. Wynnie must have been sedated. She was securely tethered to the table. The alien's genitals were hidden as the alien had his back to the video recording source. The handsome alien must have penetrated Wynnie because a moan could be heard and her arms resisted the restraints. The alien stood in place for what seemed like hours. The time line appeared and Wynnie was shocked that a half day had gone by and the alien was still penetrating her. When the alien finally withdrew from Wynnie, Stella was seen entering the room.

Stella began arguing with the handsome alien. The alien grabbed Stella by the neck. Stella squirmed as he lifted Stella's blouse and bit her on her left breast. The alien could be seen sucking blood from Stella. Stella's movements slowed. The alien dropped her to the ground. Stella was breathing frantically and her left breast revealed bite marks with blood oozing from them.

The alien leader reached into a cabinet and removed a container. He removed the lid to reveal a dark yellow material. The alien scooped up a handful of the dark yellow gelatinous and slide it into Wynnie's vagina. After returning the lid to the container, the alien returned the container to the cabinet.

Next a large syringe was removed from a drawer. The syringe had a very long needle on the end. The alien grabbed a bottle with purple fluid from a nearby cabinet. Soon the syringe was full of the purple liquid. The handsome alien walked back to Wynnie. He felt around her abdomen. After palpating her lower abdomen for a few minutes, he found the spot he was searching for and drove the needle deep into Wynnie.

The purple fluid flowed into Wynnie's body. The alien smiled as he removed the needle. He lapped up the small amount of blood that had oozed from the injection site. The alien filled the syringe once again. He walked to Wynnie's other side and again began palpating her lower abdomen. When he decided he had found the spot he was looking for, he again drove the syringe into her flesh.

Paul could see Wynnie had gone pale. "Are you sure you want to see this"? Asked Paul.
"I don't want to watch but I need to know what happened", replied Wynnie softly.
Paul slide closer to Wynnie and put his arm around her. Wynnie continued to watch as the alien again removed the syringe and suckled on the blood that oozed from the injection site.

"Rudy said he had harvested my eggs. He lied. He was using me as a breeder for his leaders offspring", stated Wynnie.

"It matters what they did to you. They have paid for the atrocities they have done with their lives. I know there is no excuse for this situation but you have a beautiful and intelligent daughter. You can't hate her for the crimes of her father", stated Paul.

The alien continued to lap at Wynnie's blood. Wynnie shivered as she watched the alien man that had raped her and impregnated her. She hated him. She was glad he was dead. The screen went dark. The view machine ascended from the floor.

"Do you want to see more"? Asked Paul.

"No. I've seen enough. I'm not sure why KY wanted me to have access to these horrible scenes", stated Wynnie.

"He wanted you to learn about alien life. I don't know if he wanted you to have closure regarding the father of your child", said Paul.

"I thought I was artificially inseminated. I didn't realize I had been raped. I don't even know how many times or how many of them....", Wynnie wretched.

KY entered the chamber and stated, "It was not meant for you to see that recording. My people are attempting to teach you our ways of life. We are not like the evil aliens" stated KY.

"Why would you have that recording where anyone could view it"? Asked Paul.

"Your daughter will soon be our new Queen. Her history is part of her heritage", stated KY.

"Queen"? Questioned Wynnie.

"Hayley is going to be your queen"? Asked Paul.

"Yes. The legend foretold of this. A female child will be the product of distance races. The child will be born after the war in which peace will be established. She will grow with her mother nearby but will forever realize her father died to end the war", stated KY.

"A legend is just a story", stated Wynnie.

"No. We have an augur who guides us. She has long foreseen the coming of your daughter and our queen", exclaimed KY.

"I'd like to meet her", blurted Paul.

"It may be arranged", stated KY.

"Really"? Asked Paul.

"Your augur is here on earth"? Asked Wynnie.

"No. She is very old. She lives on my home planet", explained KY.

"Then how can we meet her"? Asked Paul.

"Our technology is far more advanced. We can arrange a meeting", stated KY.

"So if she's too old to come here, does that mean you would transport us to your home planet"? Asked Paul.

"I don't want to travel in space", stated Wynnie.

"No one travels into space. Your image is sent to the augur and her image is sent here. You can speak directly to her image", stated KY.

"When can this meeting be arranged"? Asked Paul.

"We are meeting with her in approximately two hours. You may join us", said KY.

"Count me in", stated Paul enthusiastically.

"Do you wish to view more of our alien life"? Asked KY.

"I think I've seen enough", stated Wynnic.

Paul and Wynnie followed KY through the back entrance of the viewing room. The small group came to another room that looked like an amphitheater.

"This is where we shall meet with the augur", explained KY.

"Will my daughter be able to leave here once she is grown or finishes this growing system of yours"? Asked Wynnie.

"Yes. She has plans to leave in less than two weeks", announced KY.

"Really"? Asked Wynnie excitedly. "I was hoping for that but I didn't think it really would happen. I thought we'd be here for the rest of our lives", stated Wynnie.

"The queen will discuss her plans with you very soon", stated KY.

Wynnie was excited. In less than two weeks, they would be able to leave. Wynnie had not paid attention but had blindly followed KY. She arrived at her room without realizing how she had gotten there.

"Wow. To actually meet an alien fortune teller", said Paul.

"I will leave you both to your thoughts. Hayley will arrive later tonight", replied KY.

Wynnie had such an odd feeling. She was angry about what she had seen had been done to her by evil alien leader but was excited she would be able to leave in less than two weeks with her daughter.

"I'll need to think up some questions for her", stated Paul.

"What? Oh. The augur. Paul. Would you mind if I took a nap? This day has been a little unnerving for me", said Wynnie.

"I am sorry. It was thoughtless of me to not realize what you must be going through. Would you like me to stay and talk with you for a while? I heard talking about your problems can help you feel better", replied Paul.

"That is kind of you but I think a short rest would do me more good right now", stated Wynnie.

"Alright. But I'm right around the corner if you need me", replied Paul.

"Less than two weeks and Hayley and I can go home. I will have to come up with a plan to explain Hayley to mom and dad. We may have to fib a little and say Hayley is a friend. That means getting a place of my own for Hayley and me. Let's see, the general will have to arrange a birth certificate and paperwork for Hayley', thought Wynnie to herself.

"Mother"? Called Hayley.

Wynnie walked up to Hayley and hugged her. "I missed you", announced Wynnie surprised that Hayley looked so grown up. After watching the video of the alien women giving birth, Wynnie had suspected Hayley would have grown into a young adult.

"I'd like to talk with you if you can make the time", questioned Hayley.

"Of course I can make the time. I will always have time for you", said Wynnie with a smile.

"Before our meeting with augur, I would like to say a few things to you", said Hayley.

"You sound so serious. The augur is only a fortune teller. A gypsy at best", replied Wynnie.

"She is a very reliable source for me and my people", exclaimed Hayley.

"Your people? I'm your people", announced Wynnie.

"I will hold a very important and significant position in the society of my people. Yes, you are biologically my parent but your race and its intelligence are hundreds of centuries behind my people", replied Hayley.

"We don't need to debate any of this. In less than two weeks, we'll be leaving this place", stated Wynnie.

KY entered and said, "We need to prepare for the arrival of augur".

"Will you walk with me mother"? Asked Hayley.

"Of course. So tell me of what you been learning", said Wynnie.

"There are so many topics that I have been introduced to recently. I do not want to offend you but you would not understand most of what I have learned", said Hayley.

"I see. Is there anything you can talk to me about"? Asked Wynnie.

"You understand I have been destined to be the leader of my people", questioned Hayley.

"Yes, I've heard. Have you developed a plan on how you will keep in contact with them once we leave"? Asked Wynnie.

"Your question puzzles me", stated Hayley.

"Well, I know it would be awkward for us to explain how you look so grown up but we'll find a way", stated Wynnie.

"That is what I needed to discuss with you. I will be going to my home planet with the rest of my people", announced Hayley.

Wynnie stopped dead in her tracks. "What"? Asked Wynnie.

"I will be leaving this planet with my people in approximately ten days", replied Hayley.

"But...... you can't! You are my daughter", exclaimed Wynnie.

"Let us be rational. How would you explain me? I would not age as you humans do. My intellect is much greater than any human person on this planet. The human world locks people like me up in think tanks. They try to use our brains to service their greed or need for weapons of war. Would you really wish that type of life on me, mother"? Asked Hayley.

Wynnie grew very quiet. "I love you. I felt you grow within me. You are a part of me. How can I let you go"? Asked Wynnie.

"My people discarded emotions eons ago. Our intelligence can best guide our decisions", stated Hayley.

"You mean you can't feel emotions or you choose not to"? Asked Wynnie.

"It is as Charles Darwin explains in his theory of evolution. Adaption. Unnecessary appendages or useless parts are pushed aside and the necessary parts grow stronger to aid in survival", explained Hayley.

"So you have no idea how much I care for you? The feelings of fear I have hearing you will leave me and this planet. To never see you again or know what goes on or happens in your life", replied Wynnie.

"We will discuss this later. We must go. Augur will soon be here to talk to us", said Hayley as she began walking in the direction of the amphitheater.

"Us"? Asked Wynnie.

"Yes", replied Hayley.

Wynnie and Hayley continued to walk to the amphitheater to meet with the augur. Wynnie slowly wiped tears from the corner of her eyes.

As Hayley and Wynnie entered the amphitheater, Wynnie noticed the room was filling quickly with aliens. There were a few military personnel seated near the door.

"Looks like we will have to stand in the hall way", said Wynnie.

"Augur wants to speak to us both. Our seats are on the platform", announced Hayley as she continued to walk toward the raised platform area. Wynnie followed Hayley. Wynnie watched proudly as Hayley walked upon the platform without hesitation. Wynnie slowly followed Hayley. It was only moments later that Paul had found his way to the amphitheater. He entered the room and Hayley flagged Paul to join her on the platform.

Suddenly the room began to darkened, just as it had with the projector in the file room to produce 3-D images of people. The image of a woman appeared on the platform. The image was so clear and finely defined that it appeared as if the woman was actually there.

The woman was aged. She had gray hair and was pleasantly plump. Her garb was similar to that of the outfits African women wear. She had various earth tone colors of material with ties of orange and brown. Her gray hair was twisted up into a bun with what appeared to be antennas holding her hair in place.

The woman turned to Hayley and smiled. She then focused on Wynnie. "You will need to strengthen your heart. Your daughter's place is with her people. You must continue on in life with the help of him" announced the woman as she pointed to Paul.

The woman continued to speak. "You will be the head of your household. Your children will be plentiful. They will not have the intelligence of Hayley but will inherit much from our DNA that has passed into their mother's body during her pregnancy with Hayley. Great feats you will accomplish but only with the help of your wife and your friend....... there", stated the old woman as she pointed to Wally.

Wally blushed as all eyes focused upon him. "Great rewards will be given you for your assistance in stopping the evil ones. Our people can now return home now that all the evil ones and their off springs have been terminated. Your planet may once again grow without external threats", announced the augur.

KY came in and announced, "Hayley, augur is now your servant. Ask her to guide you with her foresight and wisdom".

Hayley stood and faced the augur. "Great augur. When shall my people and I plan our exodus"?

"When the earth's moon is quartered. The night will give you shades of darkness. It will be safe travels for you and our people", announced the augur.

"Thank you wise augur for your insight. We shall soon head toward home", announced Hayley.

KY was handed a box. He stepped near Hayley. He removed a circular item from the box and placed it on Hayley's head. It glittered with all the colors of the rainbow. Wynnie was in awe at the beauty of what must be the crown of the queen. Hayley closed her eyes. The crown began to glow. It first glowed a brilliant blue then darkened to a ruby red. The red next lightened and changed to an emerald green. The emerald green lightened and changed to a golden yellow. The golden yellow color changed to a beautiful lilac purple color then changed back to a glittering color.

"I have informed my people when we will leave. It will be a joyous reunion when we reach Trappist 1", announced Hayley.

The augur turned to face Hayley. She bowed and said, "I will prepare and await your arrival". The image of the augur began to shrink until it was only a small flickering light then it vanished completely.

Hayley turned to Wynnie and Paul. "Augur has seen your future. It is a bright future filled with many children whom you can love and cherish. It tells me you will be able to carry on without my presence", stated Hayley.

Wynnie looked sad. "It seems this life's journey still has me being the loser", whispered Wynnie.

Paul put his arm around Wynnie and said, "You haven't lost everything. You still have Wally and me".

Hayley turned to the group. "We must prepare for our journey home. Please be mindful when you leave to prevent any destruction that may alert the humans to discover our existence".

"Hayley, I don't want you to leave. I want you to meet your grandparents. I want to spend time with you. Learn about you. Let you learn about me".

"I know you. I extracted everything you have done in your entire life as well as that of all your ancestors", explained Hayley.

"What do you mean you extracted everything?" asked Wynnie.

"Each cell contains inside the DNA and RNA, the code containing the history of each of us and our heritage lineage. While I was developing in your womb, I extracted that information", continued Hayley.

"It's not fair. You can't leave. I'm your mother and I won't let you go", stated Wynnie.

"There are still several days before my people and I leave. Why don't you and I spend that time together", suggest Hayley.

"That is a great idea. Maybe I can talk you into staying here", stated Wynnie.

"That will not happen. Shall we meet for breakfast tomorrow morning? Around 0700?" asked Hayley.

Wynnie looked at Paul. "At least you can spend her remaining time here with her", stated Paul.

Paul and Wally walked Wynnie back to her room. "Do you two want to take a drive?" Asked Wally.

"As much as I would love to be out of this place, I'm really not up to it tonight. Can I take a rain check?" Asked Wynnie.

Wally gave Wynnie a hug and said, "Sure, anytime".

Paul kissed Wynnie lightly and held her. "It will turn out alright. I promise", stated Paul.

Wally and Paul left. "Let us know if you change your mind about wanting company", said Wally.

Wynnie had a sleepless night. "I'm the parent. I should make the decisions for my daughter", she thought to herself. Wynnie decided she would tell Hayley her decision when they met for breakfast. Wynnie looked at the clock. It read 0330. "Maybe I can get a short nap before having to get up", she said to herself. She yawned and closed her eyes.

Wynnie woke up with Hayley sitting at her bedside. "Oh, you startled me", stated Wynnie.

"Yes, I know. It was not my intention", stated Hayley.

"What time is it?" Asked Wynnie.

"It's almost 2:00 pm. When you failed to arrive for breakfast, I thought maybe you had changed your mind regarding spend time together" stated Hayley.

"No. I didn't sleep well. I was going to just take a short nap. I must have forgotten to set the alarm clock", explained Wynnie.

"Your dreams have revealed how troubled you are regarding your situation", said Hayley.

"My dreams? How can you...."Asked Wynnie.

"Know your dreams? I can read your mind", explained Hayley.

"You can …. Read my mind?" asked Wynnie.

"Yes" answered Hayley.

"It seems so unfair. Almost like something is being taken from me,,,,,stolen ,,,,,without my permission", stated Wynnie.

"Please dress. We will talk when you are finished", suggest Hayley.

Wynnie showered and dressed quickly. Hayley was waiting for Wynnie in the living area.

"Do we have time to have lunch together?" Asked Wynnie.

"Yes. I plan on spending everyday with you until my people and I must leave", stated Hayley.

"Isn't there rules in your people's culture regarding parental rights?" Asked Wynnie.

Hayley smiled and explained, "The intelligence of my people does not require parental rights. My people share thoughts, ideas, solutions, etc. with each other. There is a vast knowing among my people".

"There has to be a part of you that is human, isn't there?" Asked Wynnie.

"Instead of fixating on what will not be and attempts to find information to cling to, let us share time and have fruitful memories", suggested Hayley.

"Why don't you show me some of the things that you have been learning", suggested Wynnie.

"The teacher in you is always triggered by learning. Come with me. Let us see if I can't find something to trigger your interest", said Hayley.

Hayley led Wynnie around corridor after corridor. They ended up at the pods.

"I've seen your pods. KY actually had me use one", stated Wynnie.

"Did KY tell you about the incident that happened regarding one of our pods?" Asked Hayley.

"No. What happened?" Asked Wynnie.

"In transit, one of the fluid container hoses fractured. It caused a continuous leak. Unfortunately it was not detected immediately. The fluid leaked and drained into a surround area, creating a small pond. A human stumbled upon the pond, thinking it fresh drinking water. After drinking the fluid, the human filled his canteen with the fluid. Later the human realized he looked very young. The human boosted he had found the fountain of youth. It was said, many searched for this fountain. Of course, the fluid had been absorbed into the soil. It was quite amusing to hear that story", stated Hayley with a smile.

"How did the pods and fluid come into being?" Asked Wynnie.

"In ancient times, my people discovered the germs from humans were harmful. The great scientist held a meeting and developed these cleansing pods to destroy any impurities in the occupant that uses the pods. The pods were filled with regenerative fluid to restore our cells to their most efficient state. The end result is longevity, a healthier body, and our brain cells rewired. No atrophy, no strokes, no Alzheimer disease, just clear lucid minds", explained Hayley.

"You could help so many people if you shared this knowledge with humans", stated Wynnie.

"It would cause an early destruction of your people. Your world would become over-populated. Hunger for lack of enough food would occur. Wars and fighting would break out for the chance of survival. It was decided we cannot share certain information with humans", stated Hayley.

"I'm beginning to see how any help the aliens may give us must be well thought out so the help or knowledge doesn't cause harm to our existence", stated Wynnie.

"Exactly. Maybe you did absorb some alien DNA during your pregnancy", stated Hayley.

"Because I am rational? That is a little insulting", stated Wynnie.

"It just surprises me when humans exhibit intelligence above the threshold I have anticipated", explained Hayley.

Wynnie was a little annoyed at being thought of as an ignorant specie.

"I was not attempting to hurt you with my words. I will attempt to monitor my words before speaking to ensure they do not cause you sadness", stated Hayley.

"No. I guess I'm a little sensative when it comes to making humans seem so stupid or brainless", stated Wynnie.

"Your race has produced many things that my people cannot", exclaimed Hayley.

"What are you referring to?" Asked Wynnie.

"Your artist create such wonderful stories, paintings, buildings, music, etc. My people cannot participate in artistic creations. Our brains have eliminated anything except rational thought", explained Hayley.

"That is so sad", said Wynnie.

Hayley stopped. An odd expression flickered across her face.

"What are you thinking about? You had an odd expression on your face" Asked Wynnie.

"Nothing. A fleeting thought", stated Hayley.

"Keeping secrets?" Asked Wynnie.

"I read your mind. You were thinking about how you would have planned childhood activities to do with me", stated Hayley.

"I guess when you love someone, you want them to be with you. Parents like to spend time with their child or children and teach them things or create fun memories", stated Wynnie.

Wynnie saw the flicker cross Hayley's face again.

"Are you alright?" Asked Wynnie.

"Of course", replied Hayley.

"I seem to be affecting you. I don't know if it's a good thing or a bad thing", stated Wynnie.

"Do not worry. Let us continue onward", stated Hayley.

Hayley led Wynnie to a very isolated area.

"I thought you may wish to see the vehicle my people and I will use to return to our planet", stated Hayley.

"You are going to allow me to see a space ship?" Asked Wynnie.

"If you care to see one", stated Hayley.

"Of course, I'd love too. Poor Paul, he would have given his right arm to see a space ship", stated Wynnie.

"The hulls are built to withstand tremendous pressure. Our journey home requires we travel through a worm hole. We must have a ship with speed and strength", stated Hayley.

"A worm hole? I thought that was something Albert Einstein theorized. Is it real?" Asked Wynnie.

"Earth scientist are slowly learning about space, time, and travel", stated Hayley.

"Ok. So show me the inside", instructed Wynnie.

Hayley walked toward the ship. A panel moved, creating an opening.

"How did you do that?" Asked Wynnie.

"The ships are built to open the door as we approach. We maybe transporting items. It is more efficient to open the doors automatically then for each individual to stop and find a lever to gain access", explained Hayley.

"That is a pretty smart idea", stated Wynnie.

Wynnie followed Hayley inside the ship. It was huge.

"Why does it appear larger from the inside than from the outside?" Asked Wynnie.

"Technology. If you will continue to come with me, I'll show you the central area", stated Hayley. The two went to a wall that appeared to have lines on it.

"You will need to watch me closely in order to understand how to travel up to the next level", stated Hayley. Hayley turned her back to the wall and stepped very close to the wall. A pole rose from the floor. The area that Hayley stood on began to rise carrying Hayley upward. Hayley disappeared into the ceiling above.

Wynnie turned around and put her back to the wall, just as Hayley had done. A pole rose from the floor. Wynnie grabbed the pole for balance. The floor rose carrying Wynnie upward until Wynnie was now on another level.

"You did well", stated Hayley, "let us walk this way". Hayley guided Wynnie through narrow hallways. Hayley stopped at a very odd looking door. Hayley placed her hand on the wall and a panel opened. Hayley led Wynnie inside the room. A soft light glowed and illuminated the room.

Hayley moved her hands over a paneled area. The wall flickered and changed. Wynnie could see outside the ship.

"You changed the wall into a window?" Asked Wynnie.

"No. We changed the wall into a monitor. It picks up the view from outside the ship and transmits what is seen outside in here. It allows the navigators to monitor for space dreg to ensure nothing impedes our course", explained Hayley. Hayley moved her hand and the monitor returned to its original state.

"How do you eat and drink on your journey?" Asked Wynnie.

"Come. It is easier to show you than to explain", stated Hayley.

Hayley led Wynnie into another area. The walls were filled with what looked like huge holes in the wall.

"What are the holes for?" Asked Wynnie.

"Those are sleeping tubes. My people only need a horizontal space to sleep. The mattresses are air filled and fluctuate to promote a comfortable rest", explained Hayley.

"Is everyone assigned a hole?" Asked Wynnie.

"No. You take a sleep quarter when you need it and are no longer required to perform your duty", stated Hayley.

"Where do you sit and eat?" Asked Wynnie.

"There are areas that have seating. The seats come out of the walls. It is similar to bench seating. Beverages and life bars can be eaten there. We don't need to socialize in person. We can communicate via our thought processes. We have little need for luxuries", stated Hayley.

"Will you show me your food and benches?" Asked Wynnie.

"As you wish", stated Hayley as she began walking down another corridor. Hayley led Wynnie to another end of the ship. A large room with what looked like chrome wall paper on one full wall. The opposite wall had a line approximately five inches wide separating a bottom color from the top color.

Hayley walked to the chrome wall and tapped on a small square. The square opened and Hayley reached inside and removed a small bag with fluid in it.

"This is a glass of water. We tear the tab at the top corner and sip from the bag. It serves several purposes in packaging the water in bags. First we do not need the extra weight and storage for drinking cups. Secondly, we do not have water to waste washing dishes", explained Hayley.

"Is the water the only beverage you carry on these flights?" Asked Wynnie.

"No. We have a variety of beverages. They are mixed and put into a bag prior to delivery", stated Hayley.

"That is efficient. What about food? "Asked Wynnie.

"We have simple food. Life bars, a warm cereal type meal, and snacks", stated Hayley.

"That is it?" Asked Wynnie.

"The snacks are similar to your jerky, crackers, and pretzels", explained Hayley.

"It still seems sparse", stated Wynnie.

"It is only during travel time. Three weeks and we will return to our regular meals", explained Hayley.

"What are your regular meals?" Asked Wynnie.

"The same as yours. Vegetables and meat", stated Hayley.

"What type of meat?" Asked Wynnie.

"I think we need to leave the ship. My people will be loading supplies soon", stated Hayley.

Hayley led Wynnie out the way they had entered.

"I know we haven't had much time together, but I wanted to show you something", stated Hayley. Hayley led Wynnie into a room with various star charts on the wall. A table in the room was cluttered with maps.

"I've been calculating these star charts. There is a thirty minute window every two weeks that will allow a signal from my planet to travel through the worm hole to earth. I can communicate with you", announced Hayley.

"How can you do that?" Asked Wynnie.

"I can send my thoughts and you can think of what you want to say to me. I'll be able to pick up on your thoughts", replied Hayley.

"That is not really much compensation", replied Wynnie.

"It is all I can offer you. If you want to stay in touch with me", Stated Hayley.

"You know I do. I want you, not just a brief conversation here and there", replied Wynnie.

"I will continue to calculate the dates and times that the window will be open. I will give you that information before I leave", said Hayley.

Wynnie stared at Hayley. Wynnie could feel the sadness growing.

"I think I need some time to myself", Said Wynnie sadly.

"As you desire", said Hayley as she led Wynnie back to her room. Paul was waiting for Wynnie.

"You girls have a fun time today?" Asked Paul.

"We did", replied Wynnie.

"I will see you tomorrow, mother", said Hayley as she turned to leave.

"She is still going to leave. She showed me the ship she'll be leaving on. She even calculated a time when she can communicate with me. I don't want her to go", stated Wynnie.

"She actually showed you the ship?" asked Paul.

"What do you mean?" Asked Wynnie.

"She knows you are sad about her leaving. Why would she remind you that she is going?" Asked Paul.

"Maybe so I won't worry if I know she is in a safe vehicle", stated Wynnie.

"Or maybe she needs to know how much you'll miss her. She is part human after all", stated Paul.

"Do you really think that is it?" Asked Wynnie.

"Why bother communicating? She'll be gone and ruling her people. Why keep reminding you of what you lost? I think she cares and wants to please you. She feels badly she is having to leave you behind", stated Paul.

"Interesting notion", stated Wynnie.

"You know she'll probably be leaving tomorrow evening. Wally said he got word that the general was giving the media a story that the government would be doing some experiments and to expect unusual lights in the sky. I thought you should know so you can prepare yourself for Hayley's departure", stated Paul. Wynnie looked stunned.

"They said I'd have more time with her", whispered Wynnie.

"They have to leave when the calculation makes it safe for them to leave", stated Paul.

"I think I need some alone time. Do you mind?" asked Wynnie.

"I hate to see you like this. Are you sure you want to be alone?" Asked Paul.

Wynnie nodded yes. Paul could see a tear run down Wynnie's face.

"I'll be around if you need me or just someone to talk to. I even give hugs", said Paul, then he turned and slowly walked out.

"If she won't stay with me, then I will go with her", stated Wynnie to herself. Wynnie sat down and wrote her own mother a letter.

Dear Mom,

     I know this will be difficult for you and dad to understand. I am going away. I didn't want to tell you but when I went missing, I was raped. That heinous act resulted in a pregnancy. I must leave for reasons I can't discuss. I know you love me almost as much as I love you both. Please understand and try not to worry about me. If I find a way, I'll let you know how I and your granddaughter are doing. If I can't get a message to you, then know I love you and will think of you often. I know I have the best parents in the universe.

                 Love,
                 Wynnie.

Wynnie placed the letter in an envelope and addressed it to the home she'd never see again. Wynnie picked up another piece of stationary and wrote.

Dear Paul,

     By the time you read this, I will have left the earth. I plan on joining Hayley in her trip home. I'm not sure what would have happened between us if I had stayed. The idea of being with you is such a happy thought. I shall keep that thought with me and draw upon it when I feel lonely. Please forgive me for leaving without saying goodbye. Leaving you is the only regret I shall have for the rest of my life.

                 Love,
                 Wynnie.

P.S. Please mail the letter to my folks.

Wynnie placed Paul's letter in an envelope and simply wrote Paul on the outside. Wynnie took out yet another sheet of stationary.

Dear Wally,
        I don't think I have ever really thanked you for the multitude of things you have done for me. Saving my life several times, to being a very dear and caring friend.
        I plan on accompanying Hayley on her trip. Please continue to be there for Paul, as I know you have been in the past. I think he cares for me. Of course men don't always show their true feelings, so I may be wrong.
        My words cannot convey the gratitude I feel for you. I have come to care for you deeply. You will always be a special friend.
                        Love,
                        Wynnie.
Wynnie left the envelopes on her desk and fell into bed. Moments later, she was dreaming of taking a long, long journey.
        The next morning, Hayley came to Wynnie's room. "I won't be able to spend time with you today. My people and I are leaving tonight and need the time to prepare for departure", announced Hayley.
"Paul told me", replied Wynnie.
"I wanted to say good bye. It is unfortunate you will suffer such grief at my departing", stated Hayley. Wynnie tried to think of things that would prevent Hayley from knowing her plans in the event Hayley attempted to read Wynnie's thoughts. Wynnie thought of her own mother not being able to see Hayley. She thought of her dad looking sad at not being able to teach his granddaughter to fish. Wynnie saw that strange look cross Hayley's face.
"You do feel sadness. Don't you?" Asked Wynnie.

"I am attempting to interpret your thoughts. However; I am late. I must go", stated Hayley. Hayley turned back to look at Wynnie once more before leaving. Wynnie saw a tear trickle down Hayley's cheek.

Wynnie went to breakfast. Paul and Wally were in the cafeteria eating.

"May I join you?" Asked Wynnie.

"With pleasure", stated Paul. Wally stood and held out the chair for Wynnie.

"You look surprisingly well this morning", stated Paul.

"Thank you", Wynnie replied as she sipped on her coffee.

"I'm afraid to ask, but how come?" Asked Paul.

"I have to accept the things I have no control over. I may not like it, but it's the grownup thing to do", said Wynnie.

"I'm glad you finally resolved this inner conflict you had. I know it wasn't easy for you", stated Paul.

"How about having dinner with a couple of handsome guys tonight. I can arrange for an offsite meal", stated Wally.

"It's a date", replied Wynnie.

"Shall we plan on meeting at your room around seven? " Asked Wally.

"Seven it is", replied Wynnie.

"I don't want to rain on anyone's parade but isn't that about the time that Hayley will be leaving? Won't you want to say good bye or see her off?" Asked Paul.

"We have already said our good byes", stated Wynnie.

"Maybe it would be harder on Wynnie if she actually saw Hayley leave", suggested Wally.

Wynnie sipped on her coffee then looked up and said, "I don't need to see her leave. I am learning to lose. So gentlemen, are we on for dinner at seven or not?" Asked Wynnie.

"I'm in", stated Wally.

"Me too", replied Paul.

After breakfast, Wynnie gathered her letters. She placed the letters for Paul and Wally on her bed. She walked out to find her way to the ship. Wynnie saw several alien men with a cart full of supplies.

"If I follow them, they should lead me to the ship", thought Wynnie. Twenty minutes later, Wynnie stood in front of the ship that Hayley and she had stood in front of yesterday. Wynnie waited for a few minutes to give the men time to get on board and away from the entrance to the ship.

Wynnie walked toward the ship. The door opened and Wynnie entered. She walked to the wall. She turned around just as Hayley had shown her the day before and placed her back to the wall. The pole emerged from the floor. Wynnie took a hold of the pole and was soon elevated to the next level.

Wynnie walked down the hallway until she came to the area with the holes. Wynnie climbed into the first hole. The mattress inflated to make a soft comfortable bed. Wynnie noticed a button on the inside area near the entrance of the tube. Wynnie pushed on the button and a door closed the end of the tube. A pale green light illuminated the tube.

Wynnie looked around. There were two small buttons within reach at the top of the tube. "It must be an on and off switch for the lights", thought Wynnie. She pushed the button furthest from her. The lights went off. Wynnie smiled. She pushed the button closest to her. A flowery scent filled the air. Wynnie took several deep breaths. Her head felt heavy. She could barely keep her eyes open. She tried to reach for the light button but her arms felt too weak. She closed her eyes and slept.

Paul and Wally knew Wynnie would need a friend. Her daughter was leaving earth and Wynnie would never see her again. Wynnie would need support and lots of it. When Paul and Wally knocked on Wynnie's door there was no answer. "Maybe she is too upset to answer the door", stated Wally. "Maybe", replied Paul as he pushed open the door to Wynnie's room. It didn't take Paul and Wally long to find the letters Wynnie had written.

"She is going to stow away on board the space ship. We've got to get her before it takes off", stated Wally as he raced out of Wynnie's room and down the corridor. Paul followed Wally as they ran through a maze of hallways. They finally came to the entrance Hayley had led Wynnie through. Paul's breath caught when he saw the space ship.

"In the event we see anyone, we'll need to appear like we're supposed to be on board", instructed Wally. Wally led Paul toward the ship. Two other soldiers were exiting. Wally nodded at them. The two soldiers kept walking. Wally and Paul entered the ship. Paul kept looking around.

"I don't see any place Wynnie could have hidden herself", exclaimed Paul.

"Let's try the next level up", suggested Wally.

"How do we get to the next level?" Asked Paul.

"I'll show you. Just do what I do", said Wally as he went to the wall. Wally showed Paul how to use the lift. Soon Paul and Wally were both on the next level. Wally and Paul walked to the control area. Wynnie wasn't there.

"She'd be hiding. She wouldn't be in an area that will have people who would have her removed", stated Paul.

Wally and Paul continued to walk and search. They noticed a room with holes in the wall.

"What are the holes for?" asked Paul.

"Sleeping quarters", said Wally.

"She might hide in one of those", stated Paul.

"Let's check", said Wally.

Wally noticed one of the holes was closed. Wally put his finger to his lips and said, "Shhh. There must be an alien sleeping. We don't want anyone to know we are on board".

"We need to hurry this up. KY and his people plan to depart in less than an hour. If we get caught on board, you may get demoted and I me might be put in jail", stated Paul.

"We need to find Wynnie first", stated Wally.

"We may have to admit it. We may not find her in time and I am not leaving here without her", stated Paul.

"Well, I can't leave you here. I could not only lose my rank but get put in the stockade just for letting you come on board", stated Wally.

"Guess we are all staying on board then", stated Paul.

"I haven't been through the entire ship. The control center was the farthest point I had gone to up until now. I suggest if we are going to hide, we better do it quickly", stated Wally.

"I'm going to hide in one of these tubes", announced Paul.

"I may as well hide in one too", stated Wally. Paul and Wally each climbed inside a tube of their own.

"We had better close the ends of the tube or they will know we are human", said Wally.

"There is a button near the door. I'm going to push it and see if the door closes", announced Paul. The door closed and the dim light appeared in Paul's tube. Wally pushed the button in his tube and the door to his tube closed. The dim light came on. Wally pushed the button near the door again and the door of the tube opened. "Well, I've figured out the door", stated Wally. Wally closed the door to the tube once more. The dim lights came on. "I wonder if these buttons communicate with someone or cause the lights to get brighter", thought Wally. Wally pushed the button and the floral scent filled his tube. He couldn't fight the fatigue that engulfed him. He closed his eyes and slept.

Paul too had explored the buttons. The floral scent had caused him to fall asleep in mere seconds. Eight earth hours later, Wynnie began to awaken. She had not realized that while she slept, KY and his people, her daughter, Hayley, had all climbed on board their assigned space crafts and had left earth.

The worm hole would be in sight soon, and KY, Hayley, and all their people would be only weeks away from their home. It had been centuries since many of the good aliens had come to earth. It seems strange yet wonderful to be in space again. Some of the aliens had been born on earth and had never experienced space travel but had been able to know of its experience when in the womb.

Space was cold and dark and yet there was life out there. Stars and planets cannibalizing other space structures to continue life. The beauty of planets surrounded by meteors and space dust from other planets and stars that had exploded. Gravity pulling space debris allowing younger stars and planets to thrive and grow.

Wynnie was now fully awake. Her stomach growled.
"I guess I better let them know I'm on board", Wynnie said to
herself. Wynnie opened the door to her sleeping tube with her
foot. It wasn't easy but Wynnie managed to wiggle herself out
of the tube. Just as she stood up, Hayley was there.
"You shouldn't have come", stated Hayley.
"You wouldn't stay with me so I had no choice", stated
Wynnie. Just as Hayley started to leave, she stopped. She said
something to one of the crew in their alien language. The alien
pushed on the wall. A light came on and a keyboard like
device appeared in the air. The alien hit a few buttons. Soon
the doors to the tubes that held Wally and Paul began to open.
"Come out and follow me", instructed Hayley.
Paul and Wally crawled out of their sleeping tubes and stood.
They shook their heads slightly.
"That spray of yours sure packs a wallop", stated Wally.
Hayley led Wynnie, Paul, and Wally into a large room. A table
held beverages in bags and random snacks.
"Please, replenish while I speak", stated Hayley.
Wally walked up to the table and picked up a snack. "Sorry,
I'm starved. I missed dinner last night", he admitted.
Paul and Wynnie picked up a snack and beverage. Hayley
touched a panel on the wall. A bench slowly slide into place.
"Please, sit", suggested Hayley.
As the group sat and ate, Hayley spoke, "We cannot turn
around to take you back to earth. I must consider the
situation. In the meantime, you will eat here and sleep here.
We have limited pods to cleanse our bodies of your human
germs. You may watch our progress through our viewer that
is in this room. I will need to speak with Augur. She will
guide me in this dilemma".
Wynnie stopped eating and walked up to Hayley. "I won't
apologize for my decision. However; I am sorry if I am
causing you stress. I need to ask you something. Do you have
any feelings for me at all?" Asked Wynnie.

"I have explained to you regarding the Darwin theory", said Hayley.

"I understand Darwin's theory when I was in high school. I need to know if you would have a better life without me in it", asked Wynnie. Wynnie could see a funny expression cross Hayley's face.

"There it is again. That look", stated Wynnie.

"I accepted never seeing you again. I thought in time my responsibilities would keep me so busy I wouldn't think of anything personal. Yet here you are. Now I must decide what to do with my own mother", stated Hayley.

"You didn't answer my question", stated Wynnie.

"Mother, choices cannot always be made on wants or in your case feelings", stated Hayley.

"You are deflecting again", stated Wynnie.

"No one wants to live without their parents. However; I have come to terms", stated Hayley.

"So if you had a choice, you would want me in your life?" asked Wynnie.

"Yes. I would like to have my parents in my life", stated Hayley.

"Parents? There is only me", stated Wynnie.

"My father would have been a better role model for me. He was alien and very intelligent", stated Hayley.

"He was also evil", stated Wynnie.

"I will investigate the circumstances that caused him to be banished to asphalton. Until I do investigate, I will think of him in a neutral state", stated Hayley.

Wynnie could only stare at Hayley.

"Wynnie, come and eat", suggested Paul. Wynnie walked slowly back to where Wally and Paul were sitting.

Hayley arranged for the monitor to show the view of space. The beauty of space was eye catching.

"When we get close to the wormhole, you will need to be placed in a protective gel. The turbulence can be fatal to humans", stated Hayley.

"Placed in protective gel? "Questioned Wally.

"It would be similar to our purification pods but with protective gel that will absorb the extreme turbulence that is experienced as we enter the worm hole", explained Hayley.

"Does everyone have to be gelled?" asked Paul.

"No. My people have stations around the interior of the ship. An electrical impulse is sent through the walls which lock my people in place", explained Hayley.

"You what? That could be harmful. Can't electrical shocks kill you?" asked Wynnie.

"My people have a different physiological make-up then humans", said Hayley.

"But you are part human", said Wynnie.

"As you have seen by my growth process, my physiology is more like my people", said Hayley.

"Are you certain, you will be safe?" asked Wynnie.

"You three are the only ones who may be in danger. No human has ever come this far in space", said Hayley.

"Can you explain how your people can travel through space so easily?" asked Paul.

"My people developed controlled fusion. The immense power allows us to travel at great speeds", explained Hayley.

"How do you prevent a collision with meteors or space debris?" asked Paul.

"Meteors have some metals in them. Our space crafts are built with the ability to emit antimagnetic forces to the hull. This allows us to repel anything that may enter our path", explained Hayley.

A female alien entered. Hayley spoke to the female alien. The female alien looked at Wynnie, Paul, and Wally.

"Wynnie, Paul, and Wally, this is ELZ. She will be your point of contact", stated Hayley.

"What do you mean, our point of contact?" asked Wynnie.

ELZ will stay with you. She will be your contact if you have any needs that are not readily available in here. She can answer your questions. I have other duties I must attend to", stated Hayley.

ELZ stood nearby as Hayley manipulated the viewer. "This is the area of space we are currently passing", stated Hayley.

Paul and Wynnie observed through the monitor screen at the current view of space.

"Wow. It's almost like being at the planetarium", stated Wynnie. When Wynnie turned, she noticed that Hayley had left and ELZ now stood nearby.

"It is amazing. I can't believe we are here. What a story this would make", stated Paul.

As the ship traveled toward the worm hole, Paul and Wynnie were entranced with the beauty of space. ELZ and Wally were talking then ELZ led Wally into another room.

"You shouldn't have followed me. Now you will be stuck living on a strange planet", stated Wynnie.

"We are both stuck", replied Paul.

"I couldn't leave my daughter", stated Wynnie, "I know it doesn't make sense but when a woman carries her child, there is this bond that develops. I couldn't let her go off knowing I'd never see her again".

"It's because you care about people. There are some parents that abuse or have even killed their children", stated Paul.

"How awful", replied Wynnie.

"Let's change the topic. So have you thought about what it will be like on Hayley's planet?" asked Paul.

"Earth is Hayley's planet. She was born there and hopefully, one day we will both return there", stated Wynnie.

"Ok, ok. The planet we are heading for", stated Paul.

"Well, we will both be out of a job. They don't need teachers or newspaper men. I guess we'll have to find something we can do that will be productive and benefit our new world", stated Wynnie.

Suddenly, Paul and Wynnie began to float.

"Grab something to hold onto", yelled Paul as he managed to hold onto a latch for one of the cabinets.

"There is nothing to grab onto", screamed Wynnie as she floated upward. Her body spun slowly around and around. Hayley and several male aliens appeared.

"I think I'm going to be sick", announced Wynnie.

Wally and his new female alien friend, ELZ, came walking into the room.

"Why is Wynnie and I the only ones affected by the lack of gravity?" asked Paul.

"ELZ gave me a pair of gravity boots. I thought Hayley would have given you two a pair", stated Wally. Wynnie grabbed a hold of a metal latch that was on the ceiling.

"Mother, let go of that. It is a latch for an escape route", stated Hayley.

"I can't let go. I'll start spinning again", explained Wynnie. Gravity slowly resumed.

"Hey, what happened? I can stand freely again", said Paul.

"There is a temporary loss of gravity as we generate a greater increase in the antimagnetic force around the outside hull. Now my mother could fall from the significant height she is currently at", stated Hayley.

Wally raced into another area and returned with what looked like a small cannon.

"Good idea, Wally", stated Hayley.

Wally shot the cannon and a net of rope sailed across the room. The alien men picked up the edges. Wally and Paul joined in.

"Mother, you'll have to trust me. Let go of the latch. Jump toward the middle of the rope net", instructed Hayley.

"I'm afraid to", stated Wynnie.

"It's like a fireman trampoline. We'll catch you", promised Paul.

"She doesn't realize she has a great risk of dying if she continues to hold that latch. If it releases, that top area will open and we will all die", stated ELZ to Wally.

"Wynnie, you need to let go of the latch. Jump into the net. We'll all catch you", yelled Wally.

Wynnie closed her eyes and let go. A scream escaped her lips as she fell downward. She felt herself hit the ropes with a hard landing. Hayley raced to her side.

"Are you alright?" asked Hayley.

"Just a bit shaken", replied Wynnie.

"Your arm is bleeding", stated Paul.

Wynnie's elbow had a huge abrasion.

"I can't even feel it", said Wynnie.

"It's the adrenalin. It makes you hyped", stated Wally.

"Come with me. I will tend to your arm", instructed ELZ as she led Wynnie into a small room. The entire room was filled with cabinets. ELZ opened one cabinet and removed a container of what appeared to be applicators.

"Is that some kind of salve?" Asked Wynnie.

"No. It's a blend of antibiotics and a catalyst", explained ELZ.

"A catalyst?" asked Wynnie.

"The applicator is used to apply the gel, then the applicator is applied on top of the wound. The gel causes the applicator to morph into a temporary scab. When your body heals, the entire artificial covering will slough off", explained ELZ

"Amazing", replied Wynnie as she held her arm up for ELZ to care for.

"It is amazing to watch a human's reaction to something that has been around for many of your centuries", said ELZ.

"I guess we do seem rather ignorant when it comes to your knowledge", replied Wynnie.

"No. I did not mean to imply that. It is pleasant to watch a human when they learn of new things" stated ELZ.

"Oh. That is how parents feel when their children learn", stated Wynnie.

"I hope we can be friends. I do like your friend, Wally", stated ELZ.

"He is a good man", stated Wynnie.

"He has much knowledge that could benefit my people", stated ELZ.

"I don't understand that. You and your people are so far advanced from us humans", stated Wynnie.

"My people have very little knowledge of strategies for battles. Wally has much knowledge in the art of war and battles", stated ELZ.

"KY had mentioned that your people were inexperienced in fighting the evil aliens", stated Wynnie.

"So true. Humans have many things that I envy them for", stated ELZ.

"Really?' Asked Wynnie.

"Really", replied ELZ with a smile.

Paul and Wally were waiting in Hayley's room when ELZ and Wynnie returned.

"You must prepare for the worm hole", announced ELZ.

"Now?" asked Paul.

"Yes. It will take some time to prepare you", stated ELZ. Paul, Wynnie, and Wally watched as ELZ moved items in Hayley's room to one side of the room. Suddenly, alien men bought in what appeared to be three glass boxes. Almost coffin like. The boxes were lined up side by side. The men left the room briefly, but returned with four tanks and hoses similar to those that were connected to the pods.

ELZ somehow managed to arrange the hoses so they entered each of the boxes from one end. Hayley entered the room followed by two alien men carrying inflated mattresses. There was a mattress placed in each box. The alien men left after completing their task.

"If you each will lie down inside a box, we can get you secured", stated Hayley.

"How will a glass box keep us safe?" asked Wynnie.

"These are not glass. They are made up of a polymer that my people developed eons ago", stated Hayley.

Wynnie felt herself anger when Hayley used the term "her people". Paul, Wynnie, and Wally each climbed into one of the clear boxes.

"It could be interesting if we shared a box", said Paul with a wink.

Surprisingly, the mattresses were quite comfortable. ELZ helped Wally then Paul place the nose cushions and mouth pieces into place while Hayley assisted Wynnie.

As ELZ manipulated the tanks, Hayley attached the hoses. Soon Paul, Wynnie, and Wally were beginning to get sleepy. Once the trio were sedated, ELZ attached a hose to the last tank and aimed it into Wally's box. An orange foam engulfed Wally. When Wally's box was filled with the orange foam, ELZ began filling Paul's box.

The alien men returned carrying the tops to the boxes. ELZ finished filling Paul's box with the orange foam and moved the hose to Wynnie's box. Once Wynnie's box was filled with orange foam, ELZ removed the hose and carried the hose and tank from the room. The alien men placed the tops on the boxes. One of the men pulled out a small device and placed it on the area where the lid met the box on Wynnie's box. The entire lid glowed. After several minutes the man did the same to Paul's and Wally's box.

"They are safely protected now. Please return to your usual tasks. I will arrange for the boxes to be secured in place", stated Hayley. The men left. ELZ returned to the room.

"Will you need assistance securing the boxes?" asked ELZ.

"Yes. I would also like to discuss something with you", said Hayley.

The two women pulled a device from their pockets and aimed them at the bases of the boxes. The boxes began to glow. The bottom of the boxes had melted and was now adhere to the floor.

"I anticipated their travels will be safe now", stated Hayley.

"What did you wish to discuss with me, my queen?" asked ELZ.

"I picked up on an odd occurrence when you were filling Wally's box", stated Hayley.

ELZ blushed slightly.

"Can you explain?" asked Hayley.

"I cannot. There is something pleasant about being with him", confessed ELZ.

"Have you ever had that experience before?" asked Hayley.

"Never", replied ELZ.

"Has anyone else that you know ever commented that they have felt that way before?" asked Hayley.

"No one", replied ELZ.

"I have felt that pleasantness when I am near my mother. I thought it was the human genetic factor. However; if you feel it too, then there must be other rationale for the occurrence. I will consult with Augur when we arrive through the worm hole", stated Hayley.

The ship gained speed and rapidly approached the worm hole. Hayley sent out the announcement for her people to take their positions. Aliens lined most of the interior walls. An electrical impulse surged through the internal walls of the ship. All the aliens were locked into place. The auto-mechanism guided the ship toward the center of the worm hole.

Small space rocks were repelled by the antimagnetic field as the ship was tugged and pulled by the forces of the worm hole. Hayley and her people seemed unfazed by the electrical current that locked them in their chosen spot.

Hayley closed her eyes and attempted to reach out her mental energy to check on her mother. The electric current was interfering with her concentration. The ship's interior lighting dimmed as the worm hole propelled the ship faster and faster through the spirals of the magnetic field within the inner worm hole.

As the ship continued onward following the light impulse, the transverse magnetization began to spread outward. The interior lighting returned signaling the restoration of the magnetization. The energy field of the worm hole slowly relaxed allowing the ship's controls to again guide itself toward Trappist one.

The electrical charge within the ship ceased and allowed the aliens to again move freely. Hayley signaled several of her fellow aliens and ELZ to assist in the extraction of Paul, Wynnie, and Wally from the gelled boxes.

"How long were we out?" asked Wally.

"Only ten hours", replied Hayley.

"Ten hours. It seemed only minutes ago that we climbed into those boxes", stated Wally.

"It is odd that we don't feel stiff or achy", said Wynnie.

"It is the gel substance. You can move and flex but it still very protective", explained ELZ.

"I'm looking forward to learning more about your technology", stated Paul.

"We must first consult Augur on this situation", stated Hayley.

"Once we are on KY's home planet, what really can be done?" asked Wynnie.

"We shall find out when we meet with Augur", stated Hayley.

"How much longer will it take to get to our final destination?" Asked Wally.

"Less than two of your earth weeks", stated ELZ.

"I didn't realize your planet was so close to earth", stated Wynnie.

"Earth is not close to Trappist one. The worm-hole allows us to shorten our travel time by manipulating the space time continuum", stated ELZ.

"Are you speaking of Einstein's theory?" Asked Wally.

"Yes. He was one of the first earth men that was able to develop a basic theory", said ELZ.

"He was a brilliant scientist", replied Paul.

"There are many brilliant people on your planet earth", said Hayley.

"So can you explain about how this worm-hole works?" asked Wally.

"A worm-hole is a shortcut through the universe. We enter at one point similar to entering a tunnel. We exit at another point, same as exiting at the end of a tunnel", said Hayley.

"Of course, it's a bit more complicated than that. There is always the possibilities that if the materials used to initiate the worm-hole are insufficient, the worm-hole could collapse upon itself. Without knowing what may be at the other end of the worm-hole can also pose a problem. For instance, it is difficult to know if the radiation levels are too high, placing everyone in danger. Then there is always the possibility of emerging into unknown matter", explained ELZ.

"You will have to teach me more about all this. I find it very interesting", stated Wally.

ELZ seemed to glow. "I am not certain I would be a very good instructor", stated ELZ.

"I think you are", stated Wally.

Paul looked at Wynnie and smiled.

"If the queen doesn't mind, I could teach you a little bit about our technology each day. Of course, it would have to be after I complete my shift responsibilities", stated ELZ.

"I'd like that", stated Wally.

"That is an excellent idea. I was contemplating how to keep our stow-aways entertained in this one room for the next several weeks. I believe you just solved my conundrum", stated Hayley.

"Really? You wouldn't mind if we learned about your technology?" Asked Wally.

"Much of our technology will be far to advance for you but some of the more simplistic information may prove enlightening" stated Hayley.

"When can we start?" Asked Paul.

"ELZ, I am taking you off your other duties and assigning you to be our ambassador. You can arrive at 0900 and end your shift at 1800", stated Hayley.

Wally smiled. ELZ smiled too.

The days seemed to pass quickly with ELZ visiting every day and basically speaking of Trappsian history, knowledge, and philosophy. Wynnie could see that Wally was losing his heart to ELZ. Of course, Paul didn't believe it was obvious until Wally asked ELZ, "has there ever been a marriage between an earthling and a Trappsian?"

"What would make you ask a question like that?" asked ELZ.

"I don't believe our people are so different. I know earthlings are behind your people when it comes to technology but we aren't so different otherwise", stated Wally.

"Trappsians' have pushed aside emotions. Earthlings use emotions to guide their decisions. It is a very crude way to make decisions that will affect you the rest of your lives", stated ELZ.

"It's not such a bad way to live if you find the right person you want to be with", stated Wally.

ELZ smiled.

"I'm curious. How do Trappsians choose a mate?" Asked Paul.

"Augur chooses for us. Each year, those Trappsians' who have chosen it is time to begin a family, meet in the great hall. The Augur will match those who she sees in her mind's eye as being an equally contributing pair", explained ELZ.

"Is there a ceremony like on earth?" Asked Wally.

"The Augur binds them. However; the couple can refuse to pair, if the couple do not like the Augur's choice. If they chose to reject Augur's choice, they may not try again for a mate for two of your earth years", stated ELZ.

"Do any of your people ever chose someone without the Augur?" Asked Wally.

"No", replied ELZ.

"So your people, who are supposed to be so far advanced then us, and yet you aren't smart enough to pick your own mates?" Asked Wynnie.

"I suppose if you state it that way, it does seem absurd", replied ELZ.

"I didn't mean to sound so critical. It seems odd not to base your life partner on your own choice. Especially with your life expectancy", stated Wynnie.

"I see that sometimes the student enlightens the teacher", replied ELZ with a smile. Wally smiled too.

"We are almost at Trappist one. Paul, Wynnie, and Wally, you will need to remain on board until I get instructions from Augur on what I must do", stated Hayley.

"Can't we explore your planet?" asked Paul.

"I cannot allow that. Your pathogens could cause harm to my people", replied Hayley.

"Geez. We have been cooped up in this room for weeks. We are getting a little cabin crazy", stated Paul.

"This situation is of your own making. You must wait", stated Hayley.

Paul, Wynnie, and Wally looked at the monitor that gave the view of the exterior sites. The planet was of a strange color.

"They have snow", stated Wally.

"Really? I wonder if they have seasons", stated Paul.

"It would be interesting to know what kind of weather they have here", replied Wynnie.

"I'm curious regarding the types of food they eat", said Paul.

"ELZ mentioned they did have changes in the weather on the surface of the planet. I believe they ignore whatever the weather maybe because they dwell below the surface", stated Wally.

"When did she say that?" asked Paul.

"I think it was one evening when she and I were having dinner", replied Wally.

"Well, I have a few questions that have been puzzling me that I'd love to have answered", said Wynnie.

"Like what?" Asked Wally.

"Well, if alien children are raised to be good and the bad alien children had to be terminated, how did the evil aliens come to happen?" Asked Wynnie.

"In all societies, greed or power can cause the citizen to change. Is this not possible?" Asked Augur.

"Oh. You startled me", exclaimed Wynnie as she turned with a start.

"I have come to offer you my decision, if you care to hear", stated Augur.

"Please", said Paul offering Augur a seat on the bench.

"You will need to be purified. The entire population of this vessel must undergo purification and you must join them. Once your purification is complete, you will be germ free. Only then will you be able to join us in our living area", stated Augur.

"I feel awful that we had to make the entire crew go through purification", stated Wynnie.

"They would have been scheduled for purification no matter if you were on board or not because of the destination from which they arrived", explained Augur.

"Oh. Thank goodness. I thought it was my fault", stated Wynnie.

"Our people go through purification in a duration of what earth people call a year", said Augur.

"If your people are free of germs, why would you need purification every year?" Asked Wynnie.

"To prolong our life span", stated Augur.

"Will this purification process prolong our lives?" Asked Paul.

"Assuredly", exclaimed Augur.

"May I ask a question without sounding as though I'm insulting you?" Asked Wally.

"You wish to know why I look so old. The purification process works, however, when hundreds of your earth centuries have gone by, the purification process cannot keep one young forever", stated Augur.

"You are hundreds of centuries old?" Questioned Paul.

"Your planet and its life forms are very young. My people have watched your world develop and unfortunately, will be a witness to its death", stated Augur.

"What do you mean? Its death?" Asked Wynnie.

"Most earth people are very greedy. They crave power and lust to control others. You only need to see some of your world leaders to see an example of that. Unfortunately, those leaders who attempt to be fair appear weak. Greed will bring your planet much chaos", explained Augur.

"When will earth die?" Asked Wynnie showing obvious distress.

"I cannot share that date with you. My people realized we must weigh heavily potential outcomes of any information we may wish to share", Explained Augur.

"Can I ask a question? How long does one of your queens rein?" Asked Paul.

"All these questions can be answered at a later time. We must get you to the purification pods", stated Augur. Paul, Wally, and Wynnie followed Augur to the purification pods and began their process of purification.

Wally woke up to the aroma of fresh coffee. He sat up and he saw ELZ was putting items onto a plate.

"I thought I smelled coffee", stated Wally.

"You did. It is a luxury my people have indulged in since living on your planet. We managed to bring coffee beans with us. We have grown several coffee trees and plan to place an orchard in one of our growth areas", stated ELZ.

Wally noticed he was no longer in uniform but was wearing a silk shirt and silk pants. He glanced around the room. He had no idea how he had gotten into the silk outfit or how he ended up in this new room. The room had a rounded ceiling. The entire room was silver. Pictures in black frames lined the walls. There were chairs and a sofa in one area. The furniture was upholstered with black material.

A four inch line circled the top of the walls in every room. The circles emitted light.

"Come eat", instructed ELZ.

"I am kind of hungry", admitted Wally.

"You should be. You were in the purification pod for over eleven hours", said ELZ.

"Is that a bad thing?" Asked Wally.

"No. It does make you really hungry", smiled ELZ.

Wally drank the coffee and poked around at the yellow gel glob on the plate.

"It's protein. It may look unappetizing to you but it is quite healthy. It tastes similar to your eggs", explained ELZ.

Wally took a bite of the yellow gel glob and said, "They taste really good. What do you call this?" asked Wally.

"They are called glair", said ELZ.

"When I'm finished eating, will you be able to show me around? I'd like to learn more about your planet", said Wally.

"Certainly. Hayley has assigned me to be your guide and resource now that you are here", said ELZ.

Paul woke up slowly. When he sat up he saw Wynnie sitting on a chair in an adjoining room.

"How long was I out?" Asked Paul.

"Almost eleven hours", said Wynnie.

"Wow. I must have been tired. I usually only sleep about six hours a night", admitted Paul.

"Purification is like being in a womb. The fluid is warm. You sleep while all the bad stuff is somehow removed", explained Wynnie.

"How long were you out?" asked Paul.

"Eight hours. Remember, I went through the process once before", said Wynnie.

"When is breakfast? I'm starved", said Paul.

"They somehow know when we are awake and what we may need", said Wynnie.

As if right on cue, a female alien entered the room with a tray.

"Is that coffee I smell?" asked Paul.

"Yes", replied the female alien.

"I was surprised too. Apparently our coffee left an impression on these people. They are actually growing coffee trees", said Wynnie.

Paul sat at the table and sipped on the coffee.

"This is the best coffee I've ever tasted", stated Paul.

"They do seem to have a way of making everything better", replied Wynnie.

Paul gobbled down his breakfast and had three cups of coffee.

"Where are the bathrooms?" asked Paul.

"Through that archway", pointed Wynnie.

Paul excused himself. Wynnie sat and admired the simple taste of the alien people. The room was a grey color. The sofa and chairs were a rich royal blue. The picture frames were royal blue. The color scheme was very tastefully done. Wynnie stood and stared at the pictures. One picture had a woman that looked like Augur, only much younger. Another picture had a male alien surrounded by his family. The male alien looked slightly familiar. When Paul returned he said, "Let's go find where Wally is and see if we can explore this place".

Wally and ELZ were walking down the corridor leading to Paul's room when Paul and Wynnie stepped into the hallway. "ELZ is our guide. She is going to show us the coffee trees they have grown….. Among other things", stated Wally.

"If you will follow me, we need to exit the living quarters to get to the horticulture area", stated ELZ. ELZ led Paul, Wynnie, and Wally down the corridor to a great hall. "This is the great hall of honors", stated ELZ.

"What warrants an honor?" Asked Paul.

"Developing something that helps our population, an act of heroism or if you hold the position of one of our leaders", explained ELZ.

"See your people aren't very different than my people", stated Wally with a smile.

ELZ smiled and began to walk to her right. The great hall took several minutes to walk through. At the end of the great hall, ELZ turned left. The group followed ELZ. They came to another corridor and ELZ turned right. At the end of that corridor was a strange looking door.

ELZ opened the door. Chairs were inside a small area. Paul, Wally, Wynnie, and ELZ entered and sat. ELZ closed the doors and the small room began to move.

"This is our transference system", explained ELZ.

"How does it work?" Asked Paul.

ELZ smiled and said, "Always asking questions for the future stories. I cannot share that knowledge with you".

"Yes, I am guilty as charged. I keep thinking of all the different stories I could be writing and sharing with the people back on earth", stated Paul.

"Sadly, that will not happen. As new citizens you will need to be evaluated to determine your best skills so you may contribute to the benefit of the population", stated ELZ.

"New citizens. I like that", said Wally.

"How long will it be before the next ship returns to earth?" asked Wynnie.

"There are no plans to return to your earth", stated ELZ.

Wynnie blanched and said, "You mean we will be prisoners of your planet?"

"Did you believe that because you stowed away on our ship, my people should accommodate your whims to come and go whenever you wish?" asked ELZ.

"Whims? My daughter was being taken from me. I couldn't' let that happen", stated Wynnie.

"The mature decision would have been to allow your daughter to achieve her destiny. There was a way to communicate with her. She notified you of that choice. Now you expect my people to bow to your whims?" asked ELZ. Before Wynnie could respond, the transference chamber stopped.

"When we step out, do not be alarmed at the odor you may encounter. It is growth stimulating granules", explained ELZ.

When Paul, Wynnie, and Wally stepped out of the chamber, the light was bright. They began walking toward the light. There was a very strong pungent odor.

"Wow, amazing", said Wally.

"We are outside", said Wynnie in a surprised voice.

"Of course. Vegetation needs light, moisture, and air", stated ELZ.

"No, I thought we would need space suits or something like a space suit to be outside", said Wynnie.

"Trappist one is very similar to your planet earth. We use the name Trappist one because your earth scientist named our solar system Trappist one", explained ELZ.

"What is its original name?" asked Paul.

"Elysium. We, like your earth, is the third planet from our sol star", explained ELZ.

"Where is Asphalton?" asked Wynnie.

"Asphalton is the fourth planet. There is no life on the surface of the planet. Prisoners that are placed on the planet must live under the surface one hundred percent of the time", said ELZ.

"Do you have long days here?" asked Paul.

"Days?" questioned ELZ.

"On earth there are hours of light from our sun followed by hours of light from the moon", explained Wally.

"Oh. I understand. This side of Elysium is always light. To help the plants grow there are adumbration screens that cover them for ten hours", said ELZ.

"What is on the other side of Elysium?" asked Paul.

"It is always dark and cold", stated ELZ.

"I am enjoying learning about our new home", stated Wally. There were acres and acres of trees, plants, and plowed fields. So much land for horticultural that it was difficult to see where the crops may have ended.

"Do you eat meat?" asked Paul.

"Yes. We raise shoat and Sinew", stated ELZ.

"Where do they grow?" asked Paul.

"We have a paddock where they are raised", explained ELZ.

"Does everyone live underground?" asked Wally.

"No. There are domiciles on the surface. They are built with surface materials. Only couples without children may live on the surface", stated ELZ.

"Why is that?" asked Paul.

"Due to the unpredictable weather. We have sudden wind storms that can be fatal to a small child", stated ELZ.

"Does anyone ever go to the dark side of your planet?" asked Paul.

"Yes. Planned surveying excursions go there. We monitor the ice levels, the movement of the rock worms, and gather chemicals used in our purification process", said ELZ.

"Rock worms?" questioned Paul, Wally, and Wynnie simultaneously.

"Yes. On your planet you have animals that can change color, is that correct?" asked ELZ.

"Those animals are called chameleons", stated Wally.

"We have worms that look and feel like rocks but they move toward the purification chemicals. We occasionally must remove them from the area", stated ELZ.

"How do you know they are worms and not rocks?" asked Wally.

"They leave a trail behind them similar to your snails", stated ELZ.

"What do the worms eat?" asked Wally.

"Chemicals and ice", replied ELZ. ELZ lead the group through tunnels until they came to a very warm area.

"Why is it so hot?" asked Wynnie.

"This is one of the conduction tubes. Warm air is diverted from the volcanic area and assists to heat our city. We also divert cold air from the dark side of the planet known as the frigid zone. We can regulate the temperatures in various areas to ensure the most optimal temperatures for comfort or growth", said ELZ.

"What do your people do for fun?" asked Paul.

"Fun? I am uncertain what you mean. My people find satisfaction in helping our population. I suppose that may qualify as your fun definition", stated ELZ.

"Do your people always work? Don't you have any personal time to relax?" asked Wally.

"We sleep and take care of our needs", replied ELZ.

"It's not the same", stated Wynnie.

"Augur needs to speak to us", stated ELZ suddenly.

"What?" Questioned Wynnie feeling somewhat unsettled at the sudden change in ELZ.

"We must go back to the great hall", stated ELZ. ELZ led them to the transference car. Soon the group was in the great hall. Augur appeared troubled. Hayley came rushing toward the group.

"What has happened?" questioned Hayley.

"Apparently, all the evil aliens were not destroyed. We had learned that they scattered out through space. Those evil aliens that did not all go to the planet earth scattered looking for a new place to live. There are very few planets that can sustain life. We just discovered, one group of evil aliens survived and plan on returning here. They have discovered your dad and his people were terminated on the planet earth. They have decided to terminate us for eliminating him and his followers", explained Augur.

"How many ships do they have?" asked Wally.

"One", replied Augur.

"How can one ship with so few men present such a threat to your entire planet?" asked Paul.

"They plan to drop a proton ticker into the largest volcano on Elysium", exclaimed Augur.

"Why destroy the entire planet?" asked Wynnie.

"Because they have nothing else to lose", answered Wally.

"When will they arrive to Elysium?" asked Hayley.

"They were six parsecs from here when we received their intentions. That leaves very little time to prepare our people", stated Augur.

"So your plan is to leave the planet?" asked Paul.

"Yes. The proton ticker will destroy our planet by causing the explosion of the batholith", stated Augur.

"What is a batholith?" asked Wynnie.

"It is a deep and huge tunnel like structure that extends towards the inner core of Elysium. An explosion could cause a total destruction of the planet. We must try to get all of our people off the planet", stated Augur.

"How many ships do you have available for transport?" asked Wally.

"Not as many as we need to comfortably house our people", replied Augur.

"We will just have to make do. Food and beverages will be of great concern. We will need to ensure health capsules are packed. We need to begin preparation immediately", stated Hayley.

"How can I help?" asked Wally.

"We can use all of you. We need to have people keep accurate inventory of the supplies loaded on board each ship. We will need to keep an accurate tally of what we have, what is used, and calculate how long each will last", stated ELZ.

"Where do you plan to go?" asked Wynnie.

"We will need to return to earth. Your polar caps are a perfect place for my people to live until we can find another planet which meets the criteria for habitation", stated Hayley.

Wynnie tried to refrain from smiling. They would be going home and Hayley would be going with her.

Hayley looked at Wynnie and said, "It may take some time to find the right planet".

"We need to go. I will escort this group to the ships so they can begin recording the supplies", stated ELZ.

"Don't you have any type of defense system in place to protect yourselves?" asked Wally.

"We did not have the need. It wasn't until recently that we had issues with the evil ones", replied Augur.

"Do you have the means to fight off these evil aliens?" questioned Wally.

"No. Any devices that were needed for protection, were taken to earth with KY centuries ago. They remained there under your governments protection", stated ELZ.

"There is nothing you can build before they get here?" asked Paul.

"It is hardly worth the risk. If we cannot stop them, our people would be destroyed. Our time is better spent planning our departure", stated Augur.

ELZ guided Paul, Wynnie, and Wally to the ships.

"I will have inventory lists in your language so you can record appropriately", stated ELZ.

There were only twenty ships in the parking stalls.

"Will the entire population fit on these ships?" asked Wally.

"No. The elders have decided to stay. To ensure there will be placement for all the younger generations and room for supplies", stated ELZ.

"That just seems so wrong. Why does war have to take people's lives? Why is it that things can't be determined by a game of chess?" asked Wynnie.

"It is unfortunate that there must be war at all", stated ELZ.

Days later the ships were ready for their departure flights. Wally, Paul, and Wynnie were to ride on the same ship with Hayley and ELZ. Hayley had decided to override Augur's decision to remain on the planet with the rest of the elders.

"I will need your assistance in the first few centuries of being queen", stated Hayley.

Augur smiled and said, "You will do well with or without me".

"Then I choose you to come with me. I face learning my new role while having to rule in a new world and in an unplanned situation. It is only logical to have as much support as possible during this transition", stated Hayley.

"Then I shall accompany you, my queen", stated Augur.

"We may as well drink as much coffee as we can now. We won't have any while in flight", suggest Paul to Wynnie.

"I feel so badly for these people. They are peaceful and yet several bad apples can ruin their entire world", stated Wynnie.

"It is no different that Earth. We have those rulers in North Korea, Russia and even our own country that only care about themselves, great sums of money, or power. It only makes the common folks have to work harder to live or have a comfortable life", said Paul.

"I know you are right. It is still so sad that a few greedy people can make everyone else's lives so miserable", stated Wynnie.

A loud humming sound could be heard. Wally and ELZ walked up to Paul and Wynnie.

"It's time to board. I thought I'd show you which ship we shall be on", stated ELZ.

"Will we have to be gelled again?" asked Wynnie.

"It is up to the queen", stated ELZ.

Paul, Wynnie, and Wally entered the ship. ELZ escorted them to the queen's cabin.

"I need to go to my assigned area. The queen will be here soon", announced ELZ.

Hayley arrived and announced, "I have had three sleep tubes installed into my chamber for the three of you". Hayley moved the panel on the far wall to expose the sleep tubes.

"Do you need to use the facilities before entering the sleep tubes?" asked Hayley. The trio declined.

"Please remember to close the door and push the distant button on the ceiling of your tube", instructed Hayley.

"Is there a reason we have to be asleep when we leave your planet?" asked Paul.

"It is for your safety. The tubes have sensors that protect the occupant during turbulence. You are not trained for space travel. This is our way of protecting you", answered Hayley.

Wally, Paul, and Wynnie acknowledged they understood and began climbing into the sleep tubes. Hayley waited until she knew Paul, Wynnie, and Wally were asleep before signaling her staff to leave the planet.

A table with food and beverages was awaiting when Paul, Wynnie, and Wally were awakened from their slumber. "Augur has knowledge of how to initiate another worm hole which should decrease our space flight time by one of your earth weeks", exclaimed ELZ.

"How is that possible?" asked Paul.

"The worm hole we used on our way to Trappist one is a wormhole created centuries ago. Unfortunately, worm holes can become unstable and collapse without warning. We must be prepared to create", stated ELZ.

"How can you create a worm hole?" asked Wally.

"Very small metal barbs are shot out into space. Through technology, we can create an electrical impulse. We eject exotic matter into the area of the barbs. Negative energy and positive energy meet creating a whirl pool effect or in our case, a worm hole", explained ELZ.

"I still have no idea what exotic matter is, but it all seems so interesting to learn about", stated Wally.

"There is so much knowledge that your people would benefit from but unfortunately, many humans become greedy. They would use our knowledge to create wealth or power instead of sharing. The Augur can determine what we can share. Of course, I believe you would be fine knowing everything", said ELZ to Wally.

Wally smiled and said, "I am like you. People should help others. They should share. They should also do their part in society".

"Can I ask a question?" asked Wynnie.

"Of course. I am here to assist you", stated ELZ.

"Your race can read minds. Augur knew the evil aliens are planning to destroy Trappist one. Can't the evil aliens read your minds and realize their plan won't end your people?" asked Wynnie.

"Augur can block their ability. It will give us time to get to safety", stated ELZ.

"How many of your citizens are staying on the doomed planet?" asked Paul.

"Thousands", replied ELZ.

"There is no way to protect your planet?" asked Wally.

"We have been a peaceful race until recently. We have no weapons", stated ELZ.

"That is so sad", stated Wynnie.

"It is unfortunate. We must also ensure the evil ones do not follow us", said ELZ.

"That's true. If they follow us, earth will have to deal with evil aliens again", stated Wynnie.

"Yes, but we have weapons", stated Wally.

"So far, there has been no news of the planets destruction. If the evil aliens do not destroy Trappist one, it is uncertain if my people will ever be able to return home", stated ELZ.

"Why is that?" asked Paul.

"We plan to destroy the worm hole", stated ELZ.

"But I thought you could create worm holes", said Paul.

"Your earth may not have the materials needed to create a new worm hole", replied ELZ.

"When can we determine the evil ones have reached Trappist one?" asked Wally.

"Augur and the queen are the only ones who have the power to reach our people on Trappist one", said ELZ.

"The waiting is so stressful", said Wynnie.

"Augur has conveyed the evil aliens have arrived near Elysium", stated ELZ.

"Tell us what is happening", demanded Wynnie.

"It seems the evil aliens have flown their ship into the volcano", stated ELZ.

"Did it destroy the planet?" asked Wally.

"No, but it did cause the volcanoes to erupt. Black lava melted a lot of the ice. Flooding is occurring in the homes of my people", stated ELZ.

"I am so sorry", stated Wynnie.

"Augur said the evil aliens knew they wouldn't be able to survive. Given every scenario, they either would have ended back on Asphalton, or try to survive on a planet they tried to destroy. They chose to try to kill the planet of the people who had sentenced them to Asphalton. In the process killing themselves. Death was their logical choice", stated ELZ.

"Will your people who are still on Elysium be able to survive?" asked Paul.

"It is unknown at this time. The destruction is still in progress. We may not find out for quite a while given the destruction caused by the ships", stated ELZ.

Wynnie felt bad.

"Did you wish to see the creation of the worm hole?" asked ELZ.

"Absolutely", stated Paul.

ELZ escorted Paul, Wally, and Wynnie to the monitor in Hayley's room. After manipulating a small control panel, the wall turned into a pseudo window. The darkness of space was almost smothering. Distant stars and planets could be seen. Moments later, a small group of sparks appeared. They flew away from the ship into space. The sparks grew larger as they traveled.

Seconds later, what looked like a bolt of lightning appeared in the direction of the sparks. Space began to swirl.

"The worm hole is forming. We shall enter when the inside displays purple and blue hues", said ELZ.

"Do we need to be put in a box again?" asked Wynnie.

"No. Recently created worm holes do not have the turbulence of those long standing worm holes", informed ELZ.

"What can we expect when we travel through the worm hole?" asked Wally.

"Nothing more than when you fly on one of your airplanes", replied ELZ.

"Shall we watch our trip through the worm hole together?" asked Paul to Wynnie.

Wynnie nodded as she continued to watch as the worm hole grew larger and larger.

"Would you like to watch our travels through the worm hole with me? Asked Wally to ELZ. ELZ smiled and nodded yes.

Space twisted and turned. Various colors appeared out of nowhere. Thirty minutes later, the worm hole had stabilized. Blue and purple colors could be seen within the turning vortex.

Paul, Wynnie, Wally, and ELZ observed as their ship moved steadily in the direction of the worm holes entrance. Slight vibrations could be felt as the ship entered the vast opening of the worm hole.

The vibrant colors continuously changing was breath taking. The constant moving and twisting of the various colors was such an unbelievable sight.

"Is there any way we can see the area where we entered the worm hole?" asked Wynnie.

ELZ manipulated the controls and the screen view changed. The view of the next space ship entering the worm hole was seen. The turbulence significantly increased when the second ship entered the worm hole.

"Is it normal to have such large vibrations when traveling in the worm holes?" asked Paul.

"Normally there is only one ship entering the worm hole at a time. This is an unusual situation", stated ELZ.

"Didn't KY and his people enter the largest and older worm hole in multiple ships? Did they have problems with what did you call them? Elementary particles?" asked Wynnie.

"The older worm hole is more stable. I was with KY and our people when we first traveled through the older worm hole. We gave each ship enough time to get through the worm hole before the next ship would enter. The elementary particles have an intrinsic angular momentum. It may be interfering with the stability of this worm hole", stated ELZ.

"Then why aren't we using the same process that KY did now?" asked Wynnie.

"This worm hole is a temporary gate way. It is undetermined of what time duration it may have", explained ELZ.

The colors twisted and circled within itself. The vibrations grew stronger as a third ship entered the worm hole.

"How long does it take to get through a worm hole?" Asked Wally.

"Time and distance is compressed. Very similar to the wires that are bent to make that child's toy. I believe you call it a slinky. The stability of the worm hole depends on the distance being compressed and the strength of the materials to create it", explained ELZ.

The exit view of the worm hole was quickly passed. Paul, Wally, Wynnie, and ELZ continued to watch as other ships navigated through the worm hole. After the fourth ship had exited the worm hole, ELZ's face froze.

"What's wrong?" Asked Wally.

"The worm hole is collapsing. We may lose the rest of our ships", exclaimed ELZ.

"Can they go back?" asked Paul.

"They can try", replied ELZ.

Suddenly the ship lunged and dipped. Paul, Wall, and Wynnie fell to ground and landed hard. ELZ had somehow remained upright and raced over to help the trio.

As they stood, the monitor showed four ships had made it through but the worm hole had completely disappeared. No one spoke. Paul, Wally, and Wynnie looked at ELZ.

"I do not know if they survived. We must continue onward", stated ELZ.

The silence seemed to last until it was awkwardly unbearable.

Wally finally broke the dark cloud that had hung over them when he said, "In war, you have to expect casualties. It is not something we want to happen. We hope it doesn't occur. With that said, any of us could have had our ship inside the worm hole when it began to or did collapse. We all knew there are risks when at war. We can be grateful for the memories we have of the fallen and continue on with our quest in their honor".

ELZ looked proud as she watched Wally as he spoke of being a soldier.

"We are still learning how to deal with war. Thank you for clarifying", stated ELZ.

"Can we ask Hayley or Augur if they can tell us if anyone made it back?" asked Wynnie.

"Now is not the time to ask that question", stated ELZ.

"Do you or I should say, does your race mourn death?" asked Paul.

"We value life. Death occurs but is so infrequent to my people that it is difficult to logically comprehend when it occurs prematurely", Replied ELZ.

Hayley entered the room and stated, "It is good that you did not get injured when the worm hole collapsed".

"Were the other ships able to make it back out safely?" asked Wynnie.

"Yes. All but three ships", stated Hayley.

"What happens to the ships when it gets caught in a collapsing worm hole?" asked Paul.

"Paul, this is not the time to ask questions like that", said Wynnie sternly.

"It is obvious you need to know some answers to help you adjust to what just happened. I will answer Paul's question. The space stretches back into its original form, pulling and stretching anyone or anything inside with it. It is believed that any matter within would be stretched like taffy. Pulling the matter until it is mere molecules which is then absorbed by small black holes", stated ELZ.

"How awful", replied Wynnie.

"It happened so quickly. Those affected probably never knew what happened", stated Wally.

The rest of the day was filled with silence. Guilty feelings of survivor guilt had everyone quiet and sad. Even the aliens who never showed emotion seemed affected by the incident.

"I think I'll get to bed early", stated Wynnie.

"That is a good idea. I think I'll go to bed too", stated Paul.

"Coming Wally?" asked Wynnie.

"I'll be a long later. I think I'd like to have a beverage first", stated Wally.

"See you in the morning then", replied Wynnie.

Paul and Wynnie left. Wally gazed at the monitor for several minutes. ELZ stood nearby gazing at the stars and planets in the distance.

"Can I ask a question about your race?" asked Wally.

"Yes", replied ELZ.

"Is it forbidden for your people to date other races?" asked Wally.

"It is not forbidden, however we are a superior race and usually must not allow our presence to be known to the lesser species. Wherever we go we have been instructed to be civil to those in which we interact as we did with your government. We must remain vigilant to ensure we do not make ourselves known to the general public", stated ELZ.

"Have any of your people ever felt the desire to be with another race or specie?" asked Wally.

"Rudy and his group should not prejudice you against us. His people were greedy and power hungry. They had no concern for anyone", defended ELZ.

"I wasn't discussing Rudy or his group. I was just discussing your people in general", said Wally.

"I don't believe it has ever happened", said ELZ.

"From what I have learned, your people have been on earth for centuries. During that time not one of your people has been attracted to a human?" asked Wally.

"I didn't say that", replied ELZ.

"Can you explain?" asked Wally.

"My people are unable to do so many things that humans can do. Yes, we can be attracted to the skills and abilities that humans process", stated ELZ.

"I see. I guess that answers my question. I think I'll call it a night too", said Wally.

ELZ watched Wally walk away. "If only…" she thought.

The next morning Paul, Wynnie, and Wally sat quietly watching the darkness of space looming outside via the pseudo window.

"I would love to find out if aliens have seasonal depression when they travel due to the length of darkness they endure", stated Paul.

"I don't know about them but I will be happy to get back home", stated Wynnie.

"We will need to be debriefed when we get back", stated Wally.

"Debriefed. Questioned to death. I want to go home. I still need to discuss how Hayley and I will be able to work out staying in each other's lives. I have no clue what to say to my parents", said Wynnie.

"She will be busy. Orchestrating new living arrangements, researching new planets that may be inhabitable, and basically running the whole ball of wax", stated Paul.

"I know it's difficult when the parent and their children work. Trying to find a little sliver of time to spend with those you love and hold close to your heart. But we'll find a way. We have to" stated Wynnie.

"I know you hate hearing this, but debriefings are not only important but mandatory", stated Wally.

"I get that but if I am giving someone useful information, it seems I should be accommodated just a little bit", stated Wynnie.

"You shouldn't argue with Wally. He is merely trying to prepare you for when we do get home. Plus you have to remember, General McMurrer was the one who was holding you against your will. General Wirwicz has been trying to help you, us", stated Paul.

Wynnie took a deep breath. "You're right Paul", then she turned to Wally and said, "I'm sorry Wally. I didn't mean to take my frustrations out on you".

"I understand. No worries", said Wally. Wynnie walked over and gave Wally a huge hug.

"I thought you were to be with the other human male. Have you not headed Augur's prediction?" asked ELZ.

Wynnie turned with a surprised look on her face.

"We are only friends", stated Wynnie pointing to Paul and Wally, "and I don't believe in fortune tellers".

Hayley came in and said, "ELZ please join me in the command center". ELZ followed Hayley out of the room to the command center.

"Do you think something is wrong?" asked Wynnie to Paul and Wally.

"Nothing you and I have to worry about", answered Paul.

"Can you explain your actions?" asked Hayley.

"I cannot", replied ELZ.

"Augur has decided you will be in the next group to marry. She has chosen a mate for you. After we reach earth, we shall arrange the coupling ceremony", stated Hayley.

"I did not realize Augur was including me", replied ELZ.

"I asked her to consider you, given your recent exhibition", stated Hayley.

"Yes, my queen. I shall plan accordingly", ELZ replied sadly.

"You must think of him. He is human and as such has human feelings. We would not want to cause him distress", said Hayley.

"I would not want to see him unhappy", replied ELZ.

"Then it is decided", said Hayley.

"Yes, it has been decided", whispered ELZ.

ELZ returned to the room with Paul, Wally, and Wynnie.

"Is everything alright?" asked Wynnie.

"The queen has just informed me the Augur will hold the coupling ceremony when we get to earth", stated ELZ.

"Is that all. Hayley sounds so official", replied Wynnie.

"Augur has decided she will find a match for me. I am to be coupled", replied ELZ.

Wally's face turned beet red and he said, "I thought you could turn down a match".

"Yes, then I will have to wait two years to be considered again", replied ELZ.

"Why can't you choose for yourself?" asked Wynnie.

"It is not a topic that can be changed. Let us discuss other topics", stated ELZ.

"What topics?" Asked Paul.

ELZ looked out the window and said, "Black holes".

"Black holes?" replied Paul.

"Yes. Did you realize there are black holes everywhere in space?" asked ELZ.

"I've heard that scientist have spotted a black hole in the center of the Andromeda galaxy", stated Paul.

"Well, there are actually numerous small black holes scattered throughout space. They vanish for lack of nourishment. Black holes are cannibalistic. They eat anything their gravitational pull can reach", explained ELZ.

"Where did all these black holes come from?" asked Wynnie.

"They were created during the big bang", replied ELZ.

"They can last that long?" asked Wynnie.

"Yes, they can", replied ELZ.

"How is they disappear?" asked Paul.

"Hawking's radiation explains that black holes that cannot receive nourishment do not gain mass resulting in shrinking and they eventually disappear", said ELZ.

"Wow. You sure know a lot about space", stated Paul.

"I guess we all admire someone or another", stated ELZ as she looked at Wally.

The days dragged by. Wally kept more to himself than usual. Paul and Wynnie found insignificant topics to talk about. Hayley would make certain to stop by several times a day to ensure the human passengers were safe.

One afternoon, Hayley came in and stated, "I would have thought you would be watching as we head toward earth".

"Earth?" questioned Wynnie.

Paul and Wynnie raced to the monitor.

"How majestic the earth looks from space and I can't tell anyone what I've seen. I can't even take a picture", stated Paul.

"Home, sweet, home", stated Wynnie.

Wally only stared at the monitor.

Earth seemed to be just in reach when Hayley came in and stated, "We will enter earth's atmosphere tomorrow night".

"Tomorrow? Why not tonight?" asked Wynnie.

"We must approach when we have the best conditions to camouflage our ships", stated Hayley.

"I keep forgetting that earth people aren't supposed to know about you", replied Wynnie.

"Maybe in the future", stated Hayley, "I have much preparation to complete. I may not see you again until we are safely on earth".

"Wally, I'll go to the general and let him know you were trying to stop me and got stuck on board", stated Paul.

"I will explain to General Wirwicz. He will be interested in our new citizens", stated Wally.

"Do you think we can find a place for all the aliens?" asked Paul.

"It seems the aliens have had places all over the planet. I don't think there will be a problem", replied Wally.

"They look like us. I'm not sure if there is a difference with our anatomy or not", replied Paul.

"Are you thinking they could blend in with the humans of earth?" asked Wally.

"Why not? If they could, Hayley could spend time with Wynnie and you could spend time with ELZ", replied Paul.
"You forgot that human germs are harmful to aliens. You also forgot ELZ is going to be coupled", replied Wally.
"The alien scientist are brilliant. They could try to develop a vaccine to protect themselves", stated Paul.
"Maybe, you forgot, the aliens have been on earth for centuries. They didn't develop a vaccine before, what makes you think they can develop one now?" asked Wally.
"They didn't' expect to stay on earth", replied Paul.
"Do you really believe they could develop a vaccine so that the aliens can live in harmony with humans?" Asked Wally.
"I do", replied Paul.
The time seemed to drag on but the time finally came for Paul, Wally, and Wynnie to enter their sleep chambers. Paul, Wally, and Wynnie woke up in the military hotel.
"I thought you may wish to have a hot shower and some clean clothes", stated General Wirwicz.
"General, I shall submit a report before my court martial is processed", stated Wally.
"No one said you would be court martialed", stated General Wirwicz.
"Sir?" questioned Wally.
"You protected our citizens. That was your responsibility on earth or elsewhere", explained General Wirwicz.
"Thank you", said Wally with a huge sigh of relief.
"I understood the aliens have requested to hold one of their ceremonies. We have arranged for them to use the ballroom in the basement here. I need you to oversee the arrangements", said the general.
"Sir, I request to be removed from that assignment", stated Wally.

"Sorry, son. I know I can depend on you to get the job done. The ceremony is tonight at twenty hundred hours. You will need to arrange for five trust worthy fellow service men to help orchestrate this get-together. Food has been arranged. You will need to ensure there is enough seating", said General Wirwicz.

"Yes, sir", replied Wally.

The hall was devoid of any decorations. The tables and chairs were set up so each coupled pair would have a table to themselves. At nineteen thirty, the aliens chosen for the coupling, Hayley, Augur, Paul, and Wynnie entered the banquet hall. Augur and Hayley went to the front of the room. A microphone and speaker system had been set up in the front of the room. Augur had given instructions that all the aliens needed to begin acting like humans. That meant speaking to each other instead of having mental communications.

Hayley spoke first. "Those chosen for coupling will have new homes available. We will begin assimilating ourselves. It is an experiment. General Wirwicz is assisting us to settle in to our new planet. He has offered all the assistance his authority can offer.

Augur stepped forward. "Let us begin". Augur looked around the room and smiled at all the faces she saw.
"LN". A beautiful young woman came forward. "LN. I have chosen MK as your mate", announced Augur. LN smiled as MK came forward and took LN's hand in his. LN and MK walked to an empty table.
"CL". A handsome young man came forward. "CL, I have chosen OG as your mate", announced Augur. CL smiled as OG came forward and took CL's hand. They too walked and sat at an empty table.
"ELZ". The beautiful young woman who had been so helpful to Paul, Wally, and Wynnie walked up to the front of the room. "ELZ, I have chosen", and then augur paused. The room grew quiet. "I cannot chose your mate but I can request he be your mate", stated Augur.
"I don't understand", questioned ELZ.
"I believe you and that young man there", Augur pointed to Wally, "would be a good match. It must be his choice, as I cannot chose for him", state Augur.

Wally smiled and walked to the front of the room. Wally took ELZ's hand in his. ELZ smiled and the two walked to the back of the room and sat at one of the tables.

Paul and Wynnie raced to Wally's side.
"Congratulations you two. I'm so happy it all worked out. I didn't know what we would do with Wally if you were paired to someone else", stated Wynnie.

ELZ and Wally sat at a table. "I wasn't sure you even liked me", stated Wally to ELZ.

"I began having these strange behavior changes. I didn't know how to handle them", confessed ELZ.

"I was too. That night when I asked you if your people could or wanted to be with another race, I felt as though there was no chance", stated Wally.

"Are you certain you want to be with me? You were put on the spot in front of everyone", said ELZ.

"I am absolutely sure. I didn't think we had a chance to be together. I'm going to have to thank Augur" exclaimed Wally.

"Where do we go from here?" asked ELZ.

"Humans get married", stated Wally, "Is this all there is to your coupling ceremony?"

"We are officially coupled", stated ELZ.

"On this planet, we get married. We wear rings to show we have vowed to love and live with each other. We even get a license to show we are forever coupled", said Wally.

"How do we do that?" asked ELZ.

"The general will need to help us with that", said Wally.

There were fifty two couples by the end of the ceremony. The general had arranged homes for each couple. A new town had been built on government property. Initially the new town had been earmarked for military personal but the general felt it would be the perfect place to allow the new citizens of earth to live.

The general arranged for Wally to assist the alien couples to become acclimated to their new homes. Wynnie was hired to teach the aliens the ways of humans. Organic fruits and vegetables were the aliens' main staple. Wynnie would show the aliens where to shop for clothing and other necessary items.

Augur and Hayley encouraged the aliens to offer input on their new way of life. Many of the aliens enjoyed the simply life but found it tedious to speak orally then mentally. General Wirwicz granted Hayley her request to use the largest auditorium. Augur and Hayley notified all the aliens of the meeting.

"What is the meeting about?" asked Wally to Wynnie.

"I haven't a clue. I haven't even seen Hayley to even try and find out", confessed Wynnie.

"Everyone is a bit on edge", stated Wally.

"Do you think Hayley and Augur are planning on leaving earth?" asked Wynnie.

"I hope not. I am not sure what ELZ would do. Stay or leave", said Wally with a frown appearing on his forehead.

The meeting was set to occur in two nights.

"If Augur and Hayley decide for your people to leave earth. What would you plan to do?" Wally asked ELZ.

"I am uncertain. Would you ever consider leaving the earth permanently?" asked ELZ.

"Earth is my home. I was hoping you would make it your home too", stated Wally.

"I don't know what to say", said ELZ.

"I guess we should see what the meeting is about before we get into an argument", said Wally.

"An argument?" questioned ELZ.

"Yes. A fight", said Wally.

"We must fight?" questioned ELZ.

"It's a figure of speech. We would debate our points. I would attempt to convince you to agree to my way of thinking and you would attempt to convince me to agree to your way" explained Wally.

"I see", said ELZ.

Wally walked up to ELZ and said, "It may not mean anything to you but I love you. I want us to have and raise a family. I want us to grow old together".

"Grow old?" questioned ELZ.

"Yes. Live a long and wonderful life", said Wally.

"You mean age?" asked ELZ.

"Yes", stated Wally.

"Why?" questioned ELZ.

"What do you mean, why?" asked Wally.

"Why grow old?" questioned ELZ.

"That is nature. We grow old", explained Wally.

"My people don't grow old", said ELZ.

"I guess that is another topic we will need to discuss", said Wally.

The auditorium was packed when Wally and ELZ arrived. Paul and Wynnie had arrived early and saved seats for Wally and ELZ. Wynnie flagged Wally and ELZ over. "We saved you two a seat", stated Wynnie. Wally and ELZ sat and waited for Augur and Hayley to arrive.

Augur and Hayley entered the auditorium and went up on the stage. The general had set up a microphone and some chairs on the stage. Augur sat down. Hayley went to the microphone.

"My people, earth does not possess the materials we need to create a worm hole. We have three choices. The first choice is to travel in space and hope we can find a habitable planet in a timely manner or risk death in space", suggested Hayley.

The audience seemed to have a negative reaction to the first choice.

"The second choice is to live on earth. With our second choice comes many decisions. We can discuss those decisions if that choice is chosen. The third choice is to see if our fellow Trappsians can somehow collect the materials needed to create a worm hole, load a ship with those materials and return to earth to rescue us ", stated Hayley.

"Remember the population of Elysium has been reduced. We also do not know the damages that may have occurred there", stated Augur.

The auditorium was buzzing with conversations.

"Shall we vote?" asked Hayley.

Augur stood. Everyone became quiet.

"We have caused the humans of earth problems for centuries. The evil aliens and our battle with them. Yet they offer us a home and assistance to survive. It would be a great change to the life styles we know. It is a stable decisions. No potential of finding what may not be there, or anticipating a rescue that may never come", stated Augur.

"Can't there be two choices?" asked Wally.

"Explain", stated Hayley.

"Why not live here and have your people on your planet see if they can gather your materials", suggested Wally.

"You offer a good option", replied Hayley.

"My children. Do you agree to our last choice?" asked Augur. The audience bowed their heads.

"Thank you Wally", said Hayley.

"I need Augur to solve a problem I have", stated Wally.

"You…….. Need Augur?" questioned Hayley.

"Yes. Those who wish to remain on earth and live amongst us, cannot look young forever. It will cause a conflict with the humans", stated Wally.

Augur stood and said, "If we choose to blend in with the human population and become earthlings, we must choose to age and die as the human people do. If you fear death and choose not to live among the humans, then you will need to find places on earth that the humans will not find you. Like the evil aliens, you will need to live in the third realm".

"Human pathogens will destroy us within months", stated MK.

"We must develop vaccines", stated Hayley.

"We do not need to decide tonight. General Wirwicz has agreed to allow us to come back here in two days. You each can choose for yourself at that time on which path you choose to travel", stated Hayley.

ELZ and Wally looked at each other.

"I wonder what decision Hayley will make", questioned Wynnie.

Paul and Wynnie walked up to Hayley and Augur.

"Why do they need to choose one way or the other?" asked Wynnie.

"And what would we do with the children? Allow them to use the pods too? Then the children's children as well? This world would over populate quickly", stated Augur.

"How did you handle things on your planet?" asked Paul.

"Limited births. Limited couples", replied Augur.

"Just like they do in China", replied Paul.

"I'm afraid to ask", mumbled Wynnie as she looked at Hayley.

"I am going with my people. As queen I must adhere to my responsibilities", stated Hayley.

"Can't someone else be queen?" asked Wynnie.

"One does not walk away from ones responsibilities", stated Hayley.

"This is your fault. You and your crazy predictions", stated Wynnie as she pointed at Augur.

"Instead of being grateful for returning to earth and us both on the same planet, you continue to argue", stated Hayley.

"You are right. I do seem selfish" stated Wynnie as she attempted to calm herself down.

"Come on. Let me take you back to the hotel. You can call your parents. We can check with the general when you may be able to go home", said Paul.

"I don't know where home is anymore", replied Wynnie.

"You can always teach from here. You'd be near Hayley", said Paul.

"Near Hayley unless she hides with her people somewhere on earth", replied Wynnie.

"If that is her choice then she could come visit you here without any worries", stated Paul.

"That is something to think about", stated Wynnie.

ELZ and Wally drove to their home. The tension was thick. Neither spoke until they were in the house.

"I guess you have a lot to think about", stated Wally.

"We both do", replied ELZ.

"I plan on having a family. Aging and when I die, I will make room for my grandchildren", stated Wally.

"Why would you limit yourself?" asked ELZ.

"Why would you want to live forever? You'd have to go into hiding. You would get bored", stated Wally.

"There would be more time together", suggested ELZ.

"It's not how much time that counts. It is what you do with the time you have", explained Wally.

"I need to think about this", replied ELZ.

"Those who choose to use the pods will need to find a place to live without risk of discovery", stated Augur to Hayley.

"I've been researching and I believe we may need find a place in one of the canyons in the subglacial mountains at the polar cap to build our new home", stated Hayley.

"Let us wait to see what decision our people make", said Augur.

"Do you see changes in the future of our people", asked Hayley.

"Patience, my child", replied Augur.

Two days later, the auditorium was filled and awaiting Hayley and Augur. Hayley and Augur entered. The crowd grew quiet. Hayley and Augur stood on the stage facing the crowd.

"We shall have each one of you come forward and tell us what you have chosen. We will then guide you to an area for further instruction", stated Hayley.

Paul, Wally, Wynnie, and ELZ sat quietly as a line of aliens formed and one by one stood before Augur and Hayley. ELZ stood and took a deep breath. ELZ slowly walked to the end of the line.

"What did ELZ decide to do?" Wynnie asked Wally.

"She didn't tell me", said Wally sadly.

Wynnie leaned near Wally and said, "We'll all stick together no matter what".

The auditorium was empty except for Hayley, Augur, Wally, Wynnie, and Paul.

"When will we know what the results are?" asked Wynnie.

"Augur and I know the results", stated Hayley.

"And?" questioned Wynnie.

"All my people have been exploring different options. They have intermittently asked Augur or me a question", stated Hayley.

"And?" questioned Wynnie again.

"All the women and most of the men wish to set roots here on earth. They want to have families and live their lives like humans. There is one problem", stated Hayley.

"What is that?" asked Wynnie.

"We would need to administer a vaccine that would protect them from your pathogens", stated Hayley.

"Can you do that? Develop a vaccine?" asked Paul.

"We believe we can. We would need to use the fluid from the pods", stated Augur.

"To develop the vaccine?" asked Paul.

"No. As part of the vaccine", stated Augur.

"Would you have enough for everyone?" asked Wynnie.

"Yes. There are a dozen men who have chosen not to join the human population", stated Augur.

"How many women have decided not to join?" asked Paul.

"None", said Hayley, "We have all decided to blend into the human race".

Wynnie ran up to Hayley and hugged her.

"Augur and I will live together. We plan to stay here where the rest of our people are settling", stated Hayley.

"Then I will move here permanently too", stated Wynnie with a huge smile on her face.

"You would be a great help to my people. We will need someone who can be a resource to daily activities. If our women partner with a human male, they will not be given the enzymes you were given when you were pregnant with me", stated Hayley.

"Your new life will be a difficult one to learn", stated Wynnie.

"From your memories, I believe it shall be a rich life", stated Hayley.

"Where did ELZ go if she is going to stay?" asked Wally.

"To get her vaccine", stated Augur.

"I thought you had to develop it", stated Paul.

"We did. As we were talking to each of your earth's new citizens, we told each to work on a vaccine. It is being readied as we speak", stated Augur.

"Augur and I must go to get our vaccines. We shall see you tomorrow", said Hayley.

"Wally, I am so glad ELZ decided to stay", stated Wynnie.

"So am I" said Wally with a huge smile.

"I just have one concern", stated Wynnie.

"What's that?" asked Wally.

"Stella and several other women said the male aliens have deadly barbs on their penis", stated Wynnie.

Wally started laughing. Wally's laughter made Paul start laughing too.

"This isn't funny. No woman is going to want a man who may accidently cause her death during sex", said Wynnie.

"What a way to go", laughed Paul.

"Stella just told you and those other women that because she was jealous of you and them. She knew Rudy's leader wanted to mate. He chose to mate with you", stated Wally.

"What was Rudy's leader's name?" asked Paul.

"I hesitate to tell you", stated Wally.

"Why?" asked Paul.

"His name is PL. It's pronounced as Paul", stated Wally.

"Holy smokes", stated Paul.

"Exactly", said Wally.

"Geez, I'm kind of sorry I know now", confessed Wynnie.

"Me too", stated Paul.

The next morning. Wynnie woke to the scent of fresh coffee. She stumbled out of bed. Paul was sitting in the living area.

"The general wants to see us", stated Paul.

"Did he say why?" asked Wynnie.

"Nope. Said he wanted to see us in his office at 0900. Its 0800 now. You'd better hurry", stated Paul.

"Save me a cup of coffee", instructed Wynnie racing to get dressed.

Later in the general's office, the general spoke to Paul and Wynnie.

"I need you two to help name the aliens with earth names and to help them learn to become citizens", stated the general.

"I'm not sure how they will feel about having a new name assigned to them", stated Wynnie.

"They have already been informed their names would be changed to help them acclimate to earth", stated the general.

So OG became Olga. CL became Carl. LN became Lynn and MK became Mike. And on and on it went until everyone had a new first name. Last names were assigned by the government. Soon every new alien had a birth certificate, a name, even a high school or college diploma. All the legal paperwork was courtesy of General Wirwicz.

Wynnie and Paul assisted the aliens, now called the new citizens in their new homes. Some of the new citizens had been living on earth for centuries and had picked up many of the ordinary daily duties. However; most new citizens required demonstrations on faucets, refrigerators, stoves, washing machines, and driers. Thermostats were explained and an information packet was produced and given to all home owners.

Wynnie explained the currency and how shopping for groceries and household items occurred. Wynnie even offered to go with any of the new citizens when they needed to shop to ensure an easier transition.

Paul was helping the male aliens to adjust to above ground living. He discussed hat wear, sun glasses, and the need for lawn mowers and weed whackers. Paul also discussed men's role in taking out the garbage on trash collection day.

After a full day of educating the new aliens, Wynnie and Paul were walking down the main road toward the hotel. Paul and Wynnie were discussing concerns of the new citizens and if they should learn to drive cars. Paul said he would suggest a driving instructor for the new citizens to the general at the first opportune moment.

"I never realized how much we had learned growing up. It seems so basic and yet the new citizens are struggling to learn", said Wynnie.

"They are really smart people. It's just all new to them. Give them some time to get acclimated", stated Paul.

Wally's jeep was seen driving toward the main road. Wally stopped when he saw Paul and Wynnie. After parking, Wally jumped out of the jeep and said, "Keep your calendars open for Saturday the twenty seventh. Elizabeth and I are going to be married".

"Congratulations. This will be a great learning opportunity for some of the new citizens", announced Wynnie.

"I want Paul to be my best man. I know Elizabeth is going to ask you to be her maid of honor", replied Wally.

"My parents are coming in that Friday", stated Wynnie sadly.

"I insist you bring them too. Hayley needs to meet her grandparents and what a better way than at a party?" replied Wally.

"Are you sure?" replied Wynnie hesitantly.

"If you aren't there, Elizabeth may not marry me", said Wally with a laugh.

"Wow. Getting married. I never thought I'd see the day", replied Paul.

"I knew she was the one the minute I set eyes on her", announced Wally.

"I know you both will be happy", said Wynnie.

"Well, you'll need to connect up with Elizabeth to help her get the gown and things women need to get ready for a wedding", exclaimed Wally.

"Where are you having your nuptials?" asked Wynnie.

"The chapel is too small so we'll have the ceremony and the reception outside. Pray it doesn't rain", stated Wally.

"What are you going to wear? I'll need to dress in the same color", stated Paul.

"Just a black suit", replied Wally.

"Do you want to keep things pretty simple?" asked Wynnie.

"I think it's better for Elizabeth if we do things simple. Of course, later on, we'll really go whole hog if our children decide to have a big wedding", said Wally.

"Got it. Did you buy the rings?" asked Paul.

"No. That's why I stopped. Should I let Elizabeth pick out the rings or should I pick them out?" asked Wally looking at Wynnie for guidance.

"You should go together", replied Wynnie.

"Ok. Well, I'd better get going. I have more people to invite and tons to do. Wynnie, remember, tell your parents I'll be mad if they don't come", stated Wally.

"I guess I'd better link up with Elizabeth and go shopping for dresses", stated Wynnie.

"I guess we will have to teach the new citizens about bachelor parties", said Paul with a grin.

"I don't think so", exclaimed Wynnie nudging Paul in the shoulder.

Wynnie made arrangements to meet with Elizabeth and help with the wedding plans.

"Let's first shop online", suggested Wynnie as she turned on the computer.

"Online? What is online?" asked Elizabeth.

"Electronic devices that have applications or connections to places that sell items", explained Wynnie as the computer hummed to life. Wynnie stroked the keys and pictures of bridal gowns filled the screen.

"They are so beautiful", replied Elizabeth.

"We need to pick one of these dresses out for you", stated Wynnie.

"Which one should I pick?" asked Elizabeth.

"Well, I would suggest staying away from the longer dresses. You plan to have your wedding outside. Grass stains would be a problem if you wear a long dress", stated Wynnie.

"I like this one", announced Elizabeth pointing to one of the pictures. Elizabeth had chosen a simple design. The dress would come down to mid-calf. The dress was form fitting with simple lace straps.

"Would you like to look at veils or hair accessories?" asked Wynnie.

"What is a veil?" asked Elizabeth.

"A veil is more of a traditional item", replied Wynnie.

"I don't want to wear a veil. Is it mandatory?" asked Elizabeth.

Wynnie smiled, "You can have your wedding any way you want. So, no veil it is. Let's look at hair accessories".

The twelve alien men looked grim. They had chosen not to assimilate into the population of earth. None of their women had chosen to join their quest. The men readied the space ship. Because they were going to be traveling a short distance, fresh fruits and vegetables were added to their stock.

The navigator mapped out the new flight plan. The pilot gave the go ahead and the ship rumbled to life. The dozen alien men spoke with their minds. Their plan was to get settled in a hidden cavern and then assign tasks to collectively meet their goals. Their goal list was short. First, attempt to communicate with Trappist one. Second, explore chemicals on the planet in efforts to create a worm hole. Third, experiment to ensure the created worm hole was stable. If worm-hole stability was met, then an attempt to return home would be initiated.

An odd feeling was shared with the group. Would our people die out? No one knew if those who had remained behind on Elysium were still alive. Could returning now be a suicide mission? No. The group collectively thought, "We have made our choice and we will meet the challenges of our plan".

Knowing they may not leave earth immediately, the group decided to keep searching the planet for their much needed resources. Eventually they would return home no matter how long it would take them. Their fellow Trappsians may have survived and will come to earth with materials to create the worm-hole to return home.

Yes, they would need to keep watching the skies.

Wynnie was able to see Hayley almost every day.

"I always think of so many questions to ask when you aren't around", smiled Wynnie.

"What questions?" asked Hayley.

"What about the alien men that didn't want to stay? Couldn't they stay here with you?" Asked Wynnie

"They must live a hidden life. They plan to keep using the pods which will keep them young. It would cause too much conflict if they stayed. Explaining their lack of aging. They may influence those who have chosen to stay. It is not logical to have them nearby. No, they need to find a place that will keep them safe and protected. Their time will be spent trying to find chemicals that may be used to create a worm hole", stated Hayley.

"How are you getting along as a new citizen?" asked Wynnie.

"Augur and I will live together. She is actually my grandmother on my father's side. So she will tell me about my father and why he was banished to Asphalton".

"I know I should be happy for you, but when I think of your father, I get upset. I know I shouldn't because without what happened, I would have you in my life", stated Wynnie.

"I think we should change the subject. I heard Wally and ELZ, oops, I mean Elizabeth are planning a wedding", stated Hayley.

"Yes. And I am maid of honor. You will get to meet my parents at the wedding. They are arriving here for a visit that week. Wally insisted they join us at the wedding", stated Wynnie.

"I think I will like being a citizen of earth", smiled Hayley.

"There is one question I wanted to ask you", stated Wynnie.

"Ask", instructed Hayley.

"With the pods, those men could live for centuries looking for chemicals. Couldn't they?" questioned Wynnie.

"Yes. They certainly could", answered Hayley.

"How will we or the people of earth know if they find the chemicals to create a worm hole?" asked Wynnie.

"I guess we will just have to keep watching the skies", replied Hayley with a wink.

"Yes. I guess we will", stated Wynnie looking up to the skies.

FINIS

Made in the USA
Middletown, DE
28 September 2017